PENNINGTON HOUSE

TALBOT TEMPLETON

BALBOA.
PRESS

A DIVISION OF HAY HOUSE

Balboa Press books may be ordered through booksellers or by contacting:

Balboa Press
A Division of Hay House
1663 Liberty Drive
Bloomington, IN 47403
www.balboapress.com.au
1 (877) 407-4847

Because of the dynamic nature of the Internet, any web addresses or links contained in this book may have changed since publication and may no longer be valid. The views expressed in this work are solely those of the author and do not necessarily reflect the views of the publisher, and the publisher hereby disclaims any responsibility for them.

The author of this book does not dispense medical advice or prescribe the use of any technique as a form of treatment for physical, emotional, or medical problems without the advice of a physician, either directly or indirectly. The intent of the author is only to offer information of a general nature to help you in your quest for emotional and spiritual well-being. In the event you use any of the information in this book for yourself, which is your constitutional right, the author and the publisher assume no responsibility for your actions.

Any people depicted in stock imagery provided by Thinkstock are models, and such images are being used for illustrative purposes only. Certain stock imagery © Thinkstock.

Printed in the United States of America.

ISBN: 978-1-4525-2742-0 (sc)
ISBN: 978-1-4525-2743-7 (e)

Balboa Press rev. date: 01/16/2015

CONTENTS

PROLOGUE...

TODAY IS SUNDAY. IT is about seven o'clock in the morning. The sun would have just broken out over the Darling Range, east of Perth. Golden fingers of light are threading their way between the curtains of my room, forming dancing figures on the wall opposite. A few birds are starting to sing, but generally all around my house there is deathly quiet. I have had a restless night, with little sleep after three am. So I got up earlier than usual, came into my slightly cold study and booted up my computer. I have absolutely no idea why I am typing this, I have absolutely no idea who may even read it after it is finished, but I strongly feel that I am being pushed along by some extra-terrestrial force, compelling me to start writing about some of the events in my life, particularly of late, which have come as a bit of a shock to me, putting it mildly. I have never written an essay, short story or even many letters to anyone, but I will try to describe these events as clearly as I am able.

Firstly my name is Mortimer Dunbar. I am sixty years old. At the moment I am living by myself in a small old type house in Star St, Carlisle, Perth Western Australia. Since I left school at fourteen, I have worked on mines long before the use of the term FIFO was invented. After my father died, I used to catch the train up to Kalgoorlie, then hitch a ride with my mates who were also working underground. It was a long trip and very tiring in hot weather, but the pay at the end of the month made it worthwhile. Recently the company has paid for us to fly in and out, one month on and two weeks off. I enjoyed the lifestyle and never noticed the lack of female company, until one day in 1980, when I was sitting quietly in a café in William St Perth, reading the morning newspaper and enjoying a bonza cup of hot black coffee, I met Lucy. She became the first of three women who I have loved, "not wisely, but too well" (Othello. Act 5 scene 2)

Last Thursday I had an appointment with an Ophthalmologist working on the fifth floor, of a building in Adelaide Tce. Perth. One of my local GP's arranged the visit, because I didn't think my sight was as good as it had been. The Doctor was recommended as "The best in the business." Precisely at nine thirty I was called from the dark room into his office. He stood in the doorway, said "good morning" as he strongly shook my hand, and looked deeply into my eyes. He was of average height, slightly shorter than I am, at five foot eight, about fifty five years of age, thinning on top, and greying slightly at the temples. He had a commanding presence and a clear sharp voice. "You're limping" he said "I really hadn't noticed" I replied, "Sit here" he urged, "Now let me feel your knee, my goodness it is swollen, does it hurt?" "Funny you ask that, doctor" I said; "It's been like that for some time, probably a few months, but yes, I have never had even the slightest pain" "Charcot's I reckon" he demurred "Now let's look at your pupils" he said, pulling his pen torch from his pocket, "Oh yes, definitely Argyll Robinson, now for your fundus"

That's when he looked at the back of my eyes and my known world changed for ever. " You've got a salt and pepper fundus, sir" he said quietly. "This means that you have had an infection by a spirochete bug called Treponema pallidum for some time, in fact, I think that you're in the tertiary stage, and I don't think you have too much longer to go, sorry about that" "Is it that serious, Doc?" I queried. "TP been around since Columbus returned from the old world" came the reply, "and yes, it is serious stuff" he replied, looking over his glasses at me. Was this some sort of augury, I thought.

He referred me to a colleague in West Perth for some shots of penicillin G. Being told that I don't have much longer to go, struck me straight between the eyes, and I haven't been able to focus on anything else since. It has been such a shock that I have had only fitful sleep ever since. That's why I was awake so early this morning that is the reason why I feel compelled to write something down about my life. I have had a really useless life, so I dearly want to leave something behind that others may find interesting, to make amends, I suppose, and I don't want them to become an arcana.

Looking through this morning's newspaper I came across a small advertisement, describing an old folks retreat called Pennington House and I intend to look into it.

CHAPTER 1

Early Years

I WAS BORN IN 1950 in a small hamlet called Ravensthorpe, in the south east of Western Australia. I was the second child to Norman and Rose Dunbar. I was christened Mortimer after a family friend who had his left arm blown off in France during WW1.and who took up dairy farming in Denmark WA until he died. I had an elder brother, Ross, who I didn't really like. He was taller and stronger than I was, so he beat me at every sport, this included boxing, tennis, and football, until I had a really bad inferiority complex. He left home when he had finished Primary School and went off to Albany to start Secondary School, living with his Aunt Dolly, my father's sister. I never saw him again, since he did well and later moved to Perth to attend University. He was killed in an air crash whilst training to become a pilot. I think that he was only seventeen or so years old.

I went through a few years of depression. Each day was for me a struggle to get to school, which was a single room, catering for six years of Primary School. There was only one teacher, a Miss Bessie Higgins, who every day rode her pony about ten miles to the school, tying the pony up under a largish ghost gum, until three thirty when we all went home. In my grade there were only two other students, Gary Wooden and Fishy Taylor.

My mother seemed to like Ross more than me, and she herself went into a deep depression after he was killed, as I think both my mother and my father expected great things from Ross. If my mother was distant, my father was the opposite, and became my best friend. Often we walked into the surrounding bush tracking kangaroos, only to come home disappointed, as we weren't quick enough to catch one.

One day when I was about twelve or thirteen, my father took me away for a weekend of camping. He explained that he had a very strong feeling that in the small hills that surrounded the town, there were minerals to be discovered. So we searched and searched, walking miles over very rough ground. Dad explained that he had a book on minerals in Western Australia, and he read this almost every day. Later, in the local pub he befriended an old wizened man, Macca Jordan, I think it was, who also had a strong feeling about possible minerals in the surrounding hills, but he hadn't been successful in finding anything worthwhile after years of trying. He told my father that he had dug a small mine but was now dying from lung cancer after a life of heavy smoking, and he wanted to sell the mine in order to pay off some of his debts. Apparently they came to some agreement, exchanged titles and so Dad became the owner of this small mine. I think that my father was successful at getting a bank loan, as soon after he bought a utility and the two of us set out to find this mine.

This turned out to be quite difficult as we had no reliable maps, and the tracks were few and far between. After two days we found a hole in the ground, about ten feet in diameter, with a windlass sitting above it together with the drum, wire rope and bucket. We assumed that this was the mine. Together we peered into the blackness, trying to see the bottom. We threw stones in and by counting the time it took to return the sound of it hitting the bottom we tried to work out the depth. We agreed on about thirty feet deep.

Dad explained that our first job was to set up camp, get a dinner going, then get a good night's sleep, for in the morning, with a different angle of the sun, it might make it easier to see just what was at the bottom of that mine. Next day we waited until the sun was almost directly overhead at lunchtime before we could see the bottom of the mine, and quite clearly an old rusted bicycle with a damaged front wheel. Also we could see two tunnels coming off to the side of the main shaft. Dad wasn't in favour of going down in the bucket before we had secured an escape route, that is, a ladder. So we went back to Ravensthorpe, to the small general store to buy three lengths of aluminium ladder, each about ten feet long, which we bolted together when we got back to the mine. There had been a wooden ladder placed in the western corner, but now it was too dangerous to use since the wood had long been affected by dry rot and white ants. However we placed the aluminium ladder over the top of the old wooden one and we chained the top to a small but solid rock, hoping that it would hold firm and give us an escape route if anything went wrong.

Having secured the aluminium ladder, all was in place to explore what was in those tunnels. Dad said that I could have the honour of being the first down into the mine, so I climbed across the windlass and lowered myself into the bucket, holding onto the wire rope. Dad lifted the huge handle so as to release the brake, and ever so slowly I descended into the unknown. At the bottom it was so dark that Dad unscrewed one of the utility's front lights and attached it to a length of wire, then on to the battery, so that we had now a strong light shining onto the walls of the first tunnel.

Dad was so excited he couldn't wait any longer, so he gingerly came down the ladder and joined me in the tunnel. We scanned the walls with our light until we saw beads of a black metal oozing out from the softer sandstone. Then to our excitement we picked up an even larger vein of the same black metal, at least fourteen millimetres, about the width of a fifth finger wide and running upwards at least five or six feet towards the ceiling.

"its black gold" Dad muttered, slightly overcome, "It's cassiterite, sonny, stannous oxide, or tin, "My God, we've found what the old fella missed, probably on account of his poor eyesight. What a shame! Now let's go and tell your mother and come back tomorrow with some tools so that we can start to mine this stuff"

I think the year was about 1960, I was about ten, maybe eleven. Dad had been searching all those years, without having a real job or a regular income so he wasn't very popular with mum.

When we arrived home mum was nowhere to be found. Dad called "Rosie, Rosie" time after time, so he went off to the dairy to see if she had started milking our only cow, Daisy, and eventually finding her feeding the chooks and collecting some eggs. Mum greeted us icily, she was not impressed. She had years of disappointment and hardship, always trying to feed us on the smell of an oil rag. At least Dad was never bibulous and what little money he did earn, he shared it with her. What drove him on was his dreams. Dreams of finding the source of money in the dusty desert that surrounded our little hamlet. Most of the people had slowly moved away since there was no regular employment. I had not seen Garry or Fishy for months, so didn't know if they still lived around here or not.

Dad was obviously disappointed with the way Mum took the news, but he was never down for long. After dinner he showed her a piece of rock which he had secreted in his pocket. He had wrapped it carefully in some lunch paper. So he placed it carefully on the table and unwrapped it slowly, until it was exposed to the meagre light above the dining room table. "Look my dear, this is what Mort and have found at the bottom of the mine, see here that's called a seam and its tin. At the time of the Korean War it was worth a pound a pound, it's down a bit now but for us, with few overheads it is still a viable proposition"

Mum made a slight grunt, because she wasn't interested, got up from the table, collected some plates then left for the sink in the kitchen. She was about six inches taller than my father, and slightly thicker built.

She was a Daikenhart and she came from Lutheran stock in South Australia, near Nuriootpa, I believe. She had joined a touring party for the first time and that's how she met Dad, The bus broke down just outside Ravensthorpe and Dad helped the bloke at the garage to tow it into the town and then fix the problem. All in all the party needed to remain in the town for over a week, which gave Dad plenty of time to see and talk to Rosie my mum. So their interest in one another blossomed. They were married in the Lutheran Church in Nuriootpa about two years later, although Dad had never been to church before, then they moved back to Ravensthorpe to live.

Since Dad stayed away from home for long intervals, Mum had to become self-reliant. That's why she had a cow and an extensive vegetable garden which was a good way to fill in her time. She even sold some vegetables to the local grocer. However deep down she was lonely, she missed speaking German, missed the local Lutheran Church, and the people who shared similar interests. I think she always saw Dad as a dreamer, a drifter and a no hoper. All her sisters were good singers, and so in the early years she kept up her practise, each day setting up her music stand and singing elegiacally to herself or practising her scales. Slowly over the years her interest waned, until when I was about eleven or twelve I never ever heard her sing again. She too was becoming a dreamer, lost in a past world, never to return to, never to see her family again, locked in a time warp with no way to escape.

But she never lost her Faith. Each day she prayed, for over half an hour in the morning after breakfast. I am sure she prayed for her family, so far away. The letters from there getting fewer and far between. First her parents passed away, then her two sisters. She never knew her nieces or nephews, just fading photos on the side wall in the kitchen was all she had to remind her of a past life. When Ross was killed in a light aircraft accident, the news was devastating for her. She sobbed continually, while doing the dishes and looking wistfully out through the only window over the sink, out across the window box of purple petunias and beetle green geraniums, far, far, away with her thoughts.

Dad never lost his urge to mine the cassiterite. We collected some more bins, and we made a trolley on which to move the loaded bins of ore to the tray of the utility. It took about a week to fill ten bins, about three hours to load them onto the tray, and then Dad would be off, heading north towards the Battery in Kalgoorlie, about four hours away. There the ore was crushed, the dry blower separated the tin, which was weighed and Dad given a receipt which he took to an agent who paid him cash. Then he took this further down the main Street to the R&I Bank Manager who deposited half in my account, the other half in Dad's.

He always bought Mum a present, once a new frock, once a modern hat, with a wide brim and flowers in the front, another time some perfume, so he was always thinking about her. I usually stayed at the mine working, since I had no transport, but also keeping a watch out for any spivs or thugs who paid us a visit every so often, stealing our tools, or mucking them up in some way. We had a 5Kva set which provided our lighting and also powered some booby traps which we set at night time, to deter any interlopers. At least once a week it was set off, maybe by some marauding kangaroo, or other animal, but we used to think it provided us security.

I helped Dad for about ten years having no other interests than picking away at the walls, using a pickaxe or crowbar, of either number one tunnel or number two tunnel which were, by now, both three times their original length, then shovelling the debris into the bucket ready to be hauled up to ground level and onto the tray of the utility.

When I did get home for a break, which was about every three months, I noticed Mum was more morose than before. Nothing now would get her out of her deep depression. Her memory was definitely getting worse, she would forget even the simplest of things. She used to knit, because she liked it and she was very good at it. Now however, she displayed little interest in anything, and when she did try knitting again, she made mistakes, and became very agitated. Both Dad and I tried to get her to come to the mine, but she was as stubborn as a mule, and never did.

Within a year Dad, however had succeeded in getting her to live with Aunty Dolly, his sister who lived in a modest house behind the main Street in Albany. I was really sad at seeing her go, the house was now quieter than ever. Daisy, the cow had contracted Johne's disease of the joints and had to be put down, the chooks were moulting and had stick fast flees around their head and eyes and needed Vaseline which we didn't have, so Dad and I screwed their necks and burnt them and that was that. The vegetables hadn't been looked after, so we missed the fresh leaves of the spinach and celery. There was a patch, about ten feet by ten feet, which Mum had been working on recently, cleanly raked and dibbled, ready for transplanting. Most of the remaining area was now full of seeding heads of wild oats or etiolated leaves of celery and spinach. We left soon after and returned to the mine.

After about a year, Dad allowed me to travel up to Kalgoorlie, teaching me to drive, until I was thought good enough to be tested for a license in Kalgoorlie. I passed on the first try, the only certificate I had ever earned, so I felt a warm pride in myself. Also my bank account had passed one hundred thousand pounds. Dad sent money to his sister, Aunty Dolly to help her pay for mum, how much I don't know.

Back at Matilda, the name which we decided to call the mine, things went on much as they had thus far. Each day the work didn't vary much. I was now quite strong and taller than Dad, who seemed to be slowing down a little. One night after having had intruders for over a week, Dad was out patrolling the hot wire which we had erected around the perimeter, with Garry Wooden, who we found in Ravensthorpe, doing nothing as usual, so Dad offered him a job, as a security officer, which he carried out sufficiently well as to get a good wage from Dad each week.

Unknown to me Dad had a revolver. In the darkness, there was a scuffle, the gun went off and in the slight moonlight they apparently saw that Fishy Taylor was dead. Together they lugged his body over to some low bushes, and I suppose they didn't want him to be discovered. I knew nothing about this incident until one day a policeman arrived on his bicycle and started asking questions.

Two days previous, Dad said he was going to go down the main shaft in the bucket, so we swapped roles for the shift. When he was ready, I pulled on the handle to release the brake cog which fitted in between the larger main cog and the smaller one, but this time something happened, it either broke or there was something more serious inside the windlass. Alas I couldn't hold on to the handle which whorled uncontrollably, until the bucket whooshed away and smashed into the ground. At first there was silence, I was quailed, then I shouted and shouted to Dad, until at last he replied. "Legs, sonny, it's me legs, broken, both of them, and me hips, Gawd! go get help, fire brigade" I raced off to the utility, shouting out to Garry, but never seeing him.

It took about ten minutes until I reached the main road. In the haze of the distance I saw a motor cycle. The rider was wearing a yellow jacket of the police force. I stood in the middle of the road holding my arms as high as I could get them until he stopped. I screamed at him to get ropes, ladders, windlass, and he was off, so I returned to the scene.

In that short time Garry had climbed down the aluminium ladder with a rope, had tied Dad onto his back and was climbing up the ladder ever so slowly, but carefully and determinedly. I helped him climb over the top and onto safe ground. Dad had passed away. He looked so thin, so wizened, and so pale. I closed his eyes. There was blood everywhere. I held his hands, so gnarled from hard work, arthritis and old age. He had been my closest mate, my soul mate, for all these years, and now he was lifeless. I was all alone and had the job of telling mum. The firemen arrived, put Dad onto a stretcher, covered him with a tarpaulin, and that was the last I ever saw of him.

Slobbering and wiping floods of tears from my eyes, I made a statement to the police. They found Fishy Taylor's body, and took Garry into custody. I headed off to Albany. Aunty Dolly greeted me at the front door. She was instantly bereft for her brother. Mum was on the veranda, wrapped up in a knitted rug, she asked who I was, gazed aimlessly around, so I kissed her on the forehead and said goodbye. I was never to see her again.

I stayed in the house in Ravensthorpe for about a month, until the court case was convened in Albany. Garry was charged with the murder of Fishy Taylor, but he was never convicted for lack of specific evidence from that night and the charge was withdrawn. In fact the constable who took down my statement at the mine, asked the court to commend Garry for the heroic rescue of my father, Norman John Dunbar, pulling him thirty feet up the aluminium ladder, in order to be ready when the rescue team arrived. A resounding cheer went up, until the presiding Judge restored order by banging his gavel loudly on the bench.

I withdrew to the local, and found an old timer sitting quietly in the corner, and who was willing to buy Matilda from me. He got the lot, except for the utility, for a modest sum. I was relieved to get rid of it, bush map and all. I never returned there again, but drove out of town, found the Norseman Highway and headed north for a new start in Kalgoorlie. I was about twenty five years old, single and sober. German blood pulsed in my veins. I was a man.

CHAPTER 2

A New Start

GETTING A JOB AROUND Kalgoorlie wasn't easy at that time and I was very fortunate to have all that money in the bank as a backup. Having nothing else to do I drove out to Holleton in the Yilgarn mining area of WA. This area was started about the late nineteen twenties. It turned out many tonnes of tin, but the State Battery was at least eighty miles away. I camped out, lived rough and pottered around the Adelaide Queen, and the Carlo Castle mines, for two or three weeks. I picked up several pieces of cassiterite in quartz, lying on the ground, but the seams were no way near what we had at Ravensthorpe, being only about four or five millimetres wide, which made it uneconomical to mine so I returned to Kalgoorlie, sadder but wiser. The stumps of the floors, of the tents the workers used for accommodation still remain. It is rumoured that at its height Holleton had at least forty pubs. I can just imagine the sore heads that must have prevailed here, and the goings on at night time.

I also changed my name from Mortimer to plain Bill. It must have done the trick as I was interviewed, passed and short listed for a surface job at one of the biggest mines in Kalgoorlie. Doug Hetherington was the mine manager at that time and the two of us got on really well. He was a teetotaller like myself, he liked his golf and his photography. He was about fifty five years old, married and had two small children. I bought a modest but comfortable house and an old bicycle which I rode to the mine every day, as it was only about five miles away. It was too risky to drive the utility to work, as jealous louts often sabotaged any vehicle left in the car park, often putting sand or sugar into the petrol tank. It was hugely expensive to have the tank taken off and cleaned, so I just left it in the backyard, and only used it at the weekends. The years passed quickly. The first five had gone in no time, and I hadn't taken any leave, so one day I went into Doug's office to ask if I could take some time off. He, as usual was very obliging and said that I could have as much as I wanted. What did I wish to do with the leave? Probably go and have a look at Perth, as I had only been there once before. Dad was a stickler to do things correctly, so we went to the Mines Department in Wellington St, to get our Miners Right before we started mining, for all of ten pounds. Also we registered the mine site, providing the Department with our bush map. I well remember the chap on the front counter wishing us well and could hardly disguise his mirth. "Tin at Ravensthorpe!" he jeered, "Best of luck, you're real pioneers!" as he turned away trying to swallow his chuckles as best he could.

So I caught the train from Kalgoorlie down to Perth. It turned out to take about seven hours. It was a steam train, large pieces of hot coal dust blew regularly into our cabin causing great distress. The hot air was stifling, so it was a relief to get into the corridor for a break. You could always pick out the locals, since they always drank their own brand of beer. This was brewed especially for the miners who whilst working underground lost salt in their sweat, so salt was added to the beer, preventing them getting muscle cramps. Few people knew about this but happily drank the brew.

The train belched voluminous clouds of thick black smoke, climbing the hills. It put on a spurt when it had crossed onto the coastal plane, and it put on quite a performance rushing through the outlying suburbs, on its way to the main station, at Perth, aiming to arrive on time. I was not disappointed when we arrived about five o'clock, and I walked to the front of the train to thank the drivers. Inside the engine room there were just three men, the engine driver was relatively clean, since he wore a red polka dot scarf around his neck, the other two, which I took to be stokers were filthy. One was bare chested, the other wore a black singlet. Both were wet through and were drying themselves down when I arrived.

I shouted to them, but I was drowned out by the noise from within. The stokers were now opening the furnace to restock the coal, the metal door clanged loudly, steam hissed from the side of the engine, almost collecting my legs, the whistle screeched to remind passengers that they too, wanted to get home. One stoker came over to talk to me. He had a stubby firmly in his right hand, gave me a wide grin, which showed a few missing teeth, the thumbs up, and that was that. The guard's shrill whistle, the wave of a green flag, and the mighty monster huffed and puffe its way out from the platform. The driver on his left hand seat, peering forward through a dirty window, and they were gone. It was an experience that I shall never forget.

Hinds 'ill! the guard shouted as if to let us know where we were, then Bakers Well!, so we all breathed a sigh of relief. We didn't stop for the renowned meat pie, available at the station, but kept up the mad rush to get to Perth on time.

That night I slept in the Salvation Army's hostel in Barrack Street. The next morning was clear and warm, with only a few puffs of white clouds leisurely crossing the azure sky. I had a shave, washed off the grime of the train ride, had a hearty breakfast of eggs and bacon, a strong mug of coffee, and I was ready to take on the world. I had a skip in my step, as I walked into the city down Barrack Street, the people seemed friendly and jovial. I put a shilling into the tin of a street collector for the Salvation Army, "Bless you," she said, smiling. "And you too" I replied, also smiling.

Little did she know that in my inside pocket I had a small book, which if I signed a cheque, I could draw money from the bank in Kalgoorlie and even buy a house, if I wanted to.

And why not, I mused, so I did. Turning into Hay St I noticed a Real Estate Agent Office on the corner, so I went inside and asked what was the price of a modest house in Victoria Park.? About eighty thousand will get you a very reasonable place, mate came the reply. He produced a scruffy book of photos. I picked one, half hidden by a large tree in the front garden, but from what I could see it didn't seem too bad, so I produced my cheque book from my inside pocket, took a pen which was lying on the counter, and I became the proud owner of a house in Victoria Park. Sight unseen. "Come again, mate" the agent said as he handed me the front and back door keys, and I was back into the glorious sunshine for which Perth is known, all over the world.

I continued my walk slowly down Hay Street until I reached William Street, when I turned to the right, saw a nice little café, sat down facing a cathedral, from which beautiful organ music floated, ordered another coffee, grabbed a newspaper from the table opposite, and settled down to enjoy my break. Soon the coffee arrived together with a plate of toast and jam "It's on the house" the waitress said smilingly. I could not have been happier at that moment. However, my joy was interrupted by a woman sitting two or three tables away, quietly sobbing.

At first I tried to hide behind the newspaper, but the sobbing got slightly louder and it kept on going. I felt uneasy, several people got up and left. I folded the paper up, finished my coffee then went over to the youngish lady at the other table. "Hey now, things can't be that bad," I said, "Yes they are," came the quick reply. "I'm Bill," I offered, putting out my hand, "I'm Lucy, short for Lucille" she replied offering me a smallish hand holding tightly onto a saturated handkerchief. "So what's been happening?" I queried. She then stopped crying and told me the whole story about how she spent that morning in the Divorce Court in Hay St. trying to get some money out of her ex-husband, but to no avail. No one really cares, about a woman with no money to pay the silver tongued lawyers, she said

"Why did you end up divorcing?" I queried "Well it's the second time I've been there" she said somewhat bitterly, "I have married two of the most suspicious men that I have ever known, it's all been a horrible misunderstanding, they don't seem to understand anything, and now I've got nothing, I've nowhere to stay, can't take back my kids anymore." She would have gone on and on unless I had stopped her, it seemed that she had got a raw deal, trying to represent herself in a man's world, so I fell for the line, and told her that she could come and live with me in Victoria Park.

She asked me what I did, was I single or had I too, been through the Divorce Courts as we walked back to the car park and her brand new Holden sedan. It seemed that the two previous husbands were suspicious of her activities and how she seemed to be getting quite a lot of money, but not so much that she could afford a decent lawyer. We arrived at the address in Victoria Park in about fifteen minutes. Inside the house, although needing some repairs, it wasn't too bad.

Later we went shopping, which all women like doing, especially when it's not their money that is being spent. We bought beds, linen, curtains, rugs, food, sheets, blankets, the list went on and on, until the cupboards were replete. I must admit that I wasn't unhappy. To me, with no experience with women, it seemed that she was a really nice person. She seemed happy with me, and that in turn made me happy. We laughed a lot, and that evening she made a very enjoyable dinner. She produced a bottle of red wine, which she had in her car, and that helped a lot to making it an enjoyable evening.

Later when we made up the beds, she refused to sleep in the single bed in the spare room. "No way, Bill, I have never slept by myself since I was about seventeen, and now that I have met you, and I really like you, then we are going to share the double bed together, got it, OK?" I showered and then remembered that my duffle bag was still at the Salvation Army Hostel in Barrack St. She also had a shower and hadn't any pyjamas, so the two of us spent our first night together as nature had intended. When she entered the bedroom, standing against the light from the dining room, in the altogether she seemed like a goddess. She was slim, smooth and curvaceous and moved like a ballerina, gliding over the floor until she slipped between the clean new sheets and snuggled next to me. If I had owned that huge gold mine in Kalgoorlie, I could not have been happier than I was right now.

I explained that I had never shared my bed with any woman before, in the whole of my twenty seven or so years. I don't know if she believed me, but she said that was impossible, "you've got a lot to learn, Bill," she whispered, and with that she turned off the bedside lamp, rolled over and drifted into sleep, after what had been a tumultuous day in Perth.

Lucy was a good teacher and soon got things sorted out between us. My leave had expired, so I had to catch the train and report to Doug Hetherington. He said that whilst I had been away he had been thinking about promoting me to acting underground supervisor. This was indeed a very responsible job and carried with it a huge rise in salary. I jumped at the proposal, and had no difficulty adapting to supervising about twenty five men underground. I rode my bike each day to work at about seven in the morning. The men would answer the roster in the lunch room, put on their protective gear, including helmet and electric light which was attached to the front of the helmet, and then drift off to the cage which took them to the various levels. The cage took about twenty five men each trip. When the security gate in the front, closed with its usual clang, there was an eerie silence for a few seconds until with a sudden drop we were off to the depths below.

By eleven o'clock the drillers had enough holes to start putting in the explosives. The electricians came in then and wired up the whole front of the face that was being worked on that day. Then they withdrew to a safe distance, the safety siren went off, all movement stopped and it was my responsibility to make sure everyone knew the procedure. Another whistle and boom, up she went. The whole face now debris and dust. We waited until most of this had settled, before allowing the front end loaders to come in and shovel it up and dump it into the trucks that brought it to the surface.

Under my watch there were no major incidents. After the month I again caught the train back to Victoria Park for two weeks of bliss. Lucy said she had missed me terribly, and became very amorous. I had left her with adequate money, with which she bought food and clothing including some very glamorous night attire. The months ticked by. Lucy confided that she was expecting, and so after what seemed an eternity she had an eight pound six boy, whom we called Rick. I think he was named after her father or brother, it didn't matter to me as long as he was healthy. And he seemed to be as he squawked each night until after two weeks I was indeed ready to be heading down to the Perth station and on the way to those dank depths for another month. At the time it didn't seem to worry me that the two weeks of leave wasn't enough time to really bond with my little son. He remained a mother's boy, and had to relearn just who I was, each time he saw me. This was quite different to my Dad, he and I had this incredible bond that lasted until his accident. I would have dearly wished that I too, could have had the same bond with my son, but alas, it seemed that it wasn't to be.

When he was ready to go to kindergarten, I noticed a complete change had come over Lucy. We had never discussed marriage, it never seemed the appropriate time, so we drifted along, but acted as man and wife, although she kept her own name. However Rick was baptised as Rick Norman Dunbar, and this pleased me immensely. It seems that some of the mystique about me had rubbed off. She even suggested that she sleep in the single room, and that seemed to indicate that something was happening to her. Each time I came home on leave I made sure that I smelt correctly, I showered and shaved daily, even got some perfume from the chemist. I washed all my clothes, so that there were no lingering odours from the mine with its diesel fumes that seem to pervade everywhere, all to little avail. Her ardour for me was waning, yet we seemed to be on very good terms.

After almost another year I knew that something was definitely amiss, so when I arrived home on the next leave, I decided to follow her tracks to one of her closest friend's house, over a mile away. There were two vehicles outside that I recognised as belonging to FIFO workers. I quietly crept down the side drive way and peeped in through a half open window. What I saw answered all the questions that I had had since I had met her. I slinked away a broken man. What was I to do, we weren't married, so I suppose she was free to do just what she wanted. Did I have any authority over her? I had had no experience with this at all, so I decided for the sake of my little boy to do nothing and let the matter drop. It broke my heart, since I had fallen deeply in love with her, and needed her, whenever I was able to get away on leave.

So this stage of my life wasn't the happiest. I had feelings that I had never had before, jealously, anger, frustration, bitterness, plus a deep feeling that I wanted to get back at Lucy in some way. So one afternoon when the plane from Kalgoorlie arrived about an hour earlier than usual, I went with two workmates to a well-known "House on the Hill" as it was known, and I was literally blown away.

Firstly the Reception staff were very polite and professional. I filled in some forms about my health, heart, was I a diabetic? Had I been there before etc etc. Then I was taken down a long passage and into a side room. I was told that my "hostess" was to be Barbara. Now obviously that wasn't her real name, because I don't want to disclose it. Presently she entered the room. She was about nineteen, tallish, spoke beautifully, and I was quite impressed. Politely she asked me to take a shower, and pointed to where I could get a towel. In an instant I was smitten, so I made a practise of visiting room 007 as often as I could.

After three or four months, expecting to get Barbara as my "hostess" I was told that she was taking some well-deserved leave but most of her clients had changed over to a new young lady called Lidia. After the introductions I could not find any objections, so I agreed and paid the money. I met her three times at least afterwards. About September of that year, Barbara returned, and yes, there were still strong feelings for her, so I asked her if I could take her out for a coffee sometime. Her answer surprised me. She told me that she would normally very much like to, but she was busy completing her PHD in Social Science at University, and this had to be marked by November, so no way did she have the time, until the end of the year.

A few months later Doug called me into his office again and offered me a supervisor's job on another mine site north of Kalgoorlie, at a mine outside Leinster. Again it carried with it an increase in salary. I packed up my few possessions and put them onto the flattop of the utility. It was a hell of a long drive over class B roads, so I approached Doug and he agreed to a plane trip. So I flew back and forth from Kalgoorlie to Leinster each month. I had lost my desire to be with Lucy and Rick so I made excuses to stay in Kalgoorlie. One thing I got from my Dad was never accept deceit, and this was the real issue here, I felt I had been deceived badly.

After my visits to "the House on the Hill", somehow I felt better, and could handle the situation with more confidence.

So I never saw Lucy or Rick for at least six months, despite her pleading letters. One day I received a phone call from Doug asking if I would travel to Meekatharra and pick up some boxes in my utility. Doug had been so good to me that I could hardly refuse, but Kalgoorlie was a long way from Leinster, and I didn't think my utility would stand up to the very rough roads, so I requested a plane trip and getting a hire vehicle when I got to Meekatharra. This was agreed to. So within a few days I had flown into Meekatharra. Hire vehicles weren't easy to find so I had to wait for two days before one was returned. Then I drove around to an enclosure and picked up six boxes, each about three feet by three feet. Quite big really and quite heavy. I was never told just what was in them, just sign here and it was over and I was off.

From Meekatharra I drove to Wiluna almost due east, and from there it was straight south to Leinster. The roads weren't the best, so the trip was slower than usual, and very dusty. Finding the road into the mine wasn't easy and I got lost. A passing diesel tanker driver sorted me out, but about ten miles out from the mine I went over a bump in the road, probably a rock, and it upset the boxes on the flattop. I slammed on the brakes and stopped, to fix the problem. It turned out that one of the boxes had broken its restraining strap and had fallen over, so I tried to lift it back up again, but not a chance, it was far too heavy, so I slid it sideways toward the rear, hoping to get better purchase on it, but damn it, it fell off the tray and on to my left foot. I was in extreme pain, and was pinned to the bitumen, unable to lift the box or to get my foot out from under it.

Almost at passing out point, an airport vehicle passed and came to my rescue. Although the driver was only a young fellow, and not very strong he helped me lift the box off my foot and with the help of another chap from a vehicle which stopped to help, we got the damn box back onto the flattop, strapped it down and I was off to deliver the cargo. "You were very lucky" said the bloke in the store room, "Did you know the box was full of dynamite?" he asked, "No way, no one tells you anything these days," I replied, as I saw a plane landing and heading over towards us. I knew the pilot, so was able to hitch a ride back to Kalgoorlie. From there, I got a taxi to the hospital from where I was air evacuated to the Royal Perth Hospital. In the morning I had the first of four operations, it seems that I had broken every metatarsal in my foot, and from now on I was to be on compo.

I was discharged to live at home and to visit the Hospital as an outpatient. Lucy seemed to be very pleased to have me back, Rick, I'm not so sure. Lucy was able to do all the shopping while I stayed home, my foot in plaster, looking after Rick. Slowly I felt that I was making some progress with the little fella. Lucy really fussed over me, getting my crutches, when I needed to go to the bathroom, putting a pillow under my ankle when I took a nap, helping me to shower. Once she found a small container of perfume that I had inadvertently put into my trouser pocket, and immediately accused me of spending time at you know where. I could not deny it, so I took it on the chin. It seemed to make us even, because the subject was never brought up again.

Doug from the mine was always very helpful. He sent some magazines for me to read, rang up about twice each month, to check on my progress. He said that when I returned to the mine he would appoint me as a First Aid Officer, providing I had attended a course at St. John's, so this gave me something to focus on and to work for. However, Lucy's health wasn't too good, she was always tired, weak, listless and altogether not much fun. The local doctor ordered chest X Rays, blood tests, all to no avail. It was now three months since I had visited Lidia, I thought of that corridor often, my thoughts of seeing Barbara for the first time, showering, and having a coffee, before I left for home.

I noticed a hard lump coming up on my number one fella bellonga me, as PNG men refer to their penis. I went to the local doctor, but he was away, so I saw a younger bloke who told me it was because I wore heavy clothing at the mine, and it rubbed certain parts. All that was needed was some zinc ointment and it would be gone in maybe four weeks.

I wasn't impressed, but he was correct. The lesion was single, firm, round, painless, and not at all itchy. It had healed up in just four weeks, after using the ointment but it was replaced after ten days, by swollen glands in my groin. This lasted for over six weeks, there didn't seem any need to revisit the doctor, and so I just left it and got on with reading my first aid book, especially the one on muscles and their names.

Lucy now found it very difficult to get out of bed each day. She was obviously getting weaker, and had pains in her bones especially the ribs and spine. Although I had a plaster cast on my left foot I somehow was able to drive the utility, albeit slowly, so I took her to the emergency department of a large teaching hospital. At first the doctor said that there was nothing wrong with her, and was going to send her home with some aspirin, however I spied another doctor, who had something to do with my foot, so I called out to him, and asked if he would take a look at Lucy.

I know that he wasn't too happy about it, made all sorts of excuses, until I lauded him for what he had done for me, and he then agreed. After he had a look at Lucy, he came over to me and said, "Well she has definitely got bad pains in her ribs and low down in her back. Have you been beating her up?" "Doc," I replied, she is so weak, she has lost a lot of weight over the last month and I feel that she has a low grade fever, as well, that no way would I do that, fair go mate." "Well she has to be admitted, but I just don't know where, maybe we'll put her in a temporary holding ward until we can run some tests." And with that he was off, quickly, as if I had held him up.

Three days later, whilst I was visiting her, a senior doctor came in the cubicle to see her. He introduced himself, sat on the side of the bed, adjusted his glasses, coughed nervously, and said you have an interesting blood picture, Mrs Dunbar. "Lucy replied that she wasn't really Mrs Dunbar, but because my name was on her records as the next of kin, everyone assumed that we were married, so the doctor took out his pen and altered the front of her file.

"What do you mean, she has an interesting blood picture, doctor?" I asked "Well, we in the haematology department just can't work it out, so we've sent some slides of her blood off to other hospitals to ask for some more opinions, so far all I can tell you is that she has some hairy plasma cells, and some anaemia, which accounts for her extreme lethargy. Her blood is also in high in calcium, it's a complex situation. Anyway we'll get some urine tests and see what evolves." He slid off the bed, adjusted his glasses for the umpteenth time, smiled and left.

Two days later we met again in the tiny cubicle which was her temporary accommodation. Again he sat on the side of the bed, adjusted his glasses, and coughed. "I have some good news for you both" he said "you should be able to go home and come back each day as an outpatient. I have started a program on my computer. It is so interesting. It is graph of your progress, there is a red line for your urinary creatinine, a blue line for your red blood count, a yellow line for the white cell count, platelets, I am not sure what colour we'll pick for that, and so he went on, talking about his computer and all the graphs

"She is not getting any better, doctor "I said, "See here, she now has bruising on the back on her hand, I really am not happy to take her home," "Oh well then, let's leave her in for a few more days, but we are really overstretched here lately, and I must discharge her just as soon as we can. And by the way, I have asked for a bone biopsy to be done this afternoon. It's quite simple really, either your sternum or your hip, I will leave it to one of the younger chaps," he said and with a quick smile he was out the door, before I was able to ask any more questions.

This was indeed a difficult time for me. Fortunately Kate, Lucy's sister took care of young Rick. She had three children of her own so she didn't lack experience. I was due to have the plaster taken off, more x rays, more blood tests, a new plaster, another operation planned for, in just over a month. This, plus all the shopping, every three days put me under a big strain, but so far I was coping. Lucy had several transfusions and was feeling much better, in fact she went for a short walk each day.

After a few weeks, there was no more talk about her coming home. She was in for the long haul. Her days were taken up with more transfusions, blood tests, urine tests and dialysis every four days, as she had kidney failure. One day she told me she felt bloated. I reported it to the senior doctor, he went pale, and asked if I was trying to interfere with her management. I told him that whilst I was on compo after my accident, I was studying for my first aid certificate. "Harrumph", was all he could reply, and kept shovelling the pathology reports, continually adjusting his glasses, and coughing, whilst punching the results into his computer. "Platelets are up' 'he muttered, as I left the room. Lucy was asleep.

Sometime later, whilst she was shuffling, along the corridors, she felt giddy and unsteady, so quickly grabbed a hand rail, and got back to her bed as quickly as she could. The resident doctor, who had been studying the case intensely, was called and suddenly rang a surgeon, poor Lucy had an emergency operation that night to relieve pressure on her spinal cord. I saw the senior doctor in the passage one day. "How is she doing?" I enquired, "really well" came the reply as he moved on quickly, probably to avoid any further questions. He must have had a lot on his mind, and more pathology reports to record on his computer.

One afternoon I found Lucy in the sunroom all by herself. Everywhere was quiet, the staff too must have been away for a break. So we sat together, holding hands and reminiscing on how we met. She told me why she thought her previous husbands had not understood her, and just how different I was to them. Lucy said that I was a real support to her, I didn't ask too many questions, never caused an argument, she said that we could get married after she got better and was home again, after all we had a child to look after, and that was important. She whispered she loved me, took a deep breath, made a little gasp, fell backwards into her chair, and stopped breathing.

I shouted for help, but none came. I went berserk, I wanted to squeeze her chest, but feared I might do more damage. Too late anyway, she was gone, despite being told she was doing alright. I was distraught, vengeful, aggressive, belligerent, and fell back into the deep depression I had many years ago. At night, all alone I started smashing things up, chairs, dishes, windows, curtains and worse of all I started drinking, beer at first then heavier stuff, whiskey, brandy, anything I could get my hands on. My foot was giving me hell, I ate too many hamburgers and pies. I became a fat slob. I was working my frustrations out, and was so disappointed that we never got married, we had missed our chance, for ever, and I started to search my computer for another woman, with whom I just may be compatible.

About six or seven weeks later, when I was coming out of my alcoholic haze, I received a letter from the Hospital, informing me of the post mortem results. It appears that Lucy had had deep vein thrombosis, that is clots in her legs, and when she took a deep breath it helped the clot to break off and become an embolus, and hence it travelled to her lungs, causing her demise. She also had cancer of her plasma cells. The treatment was, I think too late to be of any benefit.

I screwed the letter up and returned to the kitchen. Dishes had been piling up, and there was an unpleasant miasmic smell. I opened the small window. Fresh air pervaded the room, it was a new day and I had better put on my new brogues, go for a walk and enjoy it.

CHAPTER 3

Here We Go Again

IN A MAGAZINE I was reading, whilst waiting for the dentist to de tartar my teeth, I read that a Chinese philosopher once wrote, a long time ago, that a man needed a woman in his life to keep him on the right path, and to stop him straying into doing dumb things. I thought about this profound statement for a long time, especially at night when I was at my most lonely. In time I agreed with this wisdom, and started thinking of just how I was to meet another woman. Should I return to the café in William Street, order a strong black, grab a paper from another table, and wait until I heard the soft sobbing's of a distraught victim of the Divorce Court. The idea lacked immediate appeal, so I asked a neighbour how to use the Internet to log onto some sites used especially by some international lonely hearts, like me.

I scanned the UK but without success. I then scanned Germany. There were some very nice ladies with whom I corresponded for quite a while, but slowly they drifted away, and I had to enter Scandinavia. I was overwhelmed with the responses, and it was difficult to sort them out. It was now about November, my foot was at last almost better, no more operations were planned, and I was out of the plaster cast, and walking only with the aid of a stick. There was no need to return to the mine, the exam in First Aid wasn't until the first week in December, I was able to spend a lot of time each day logging into the internet and corresponding with these ladies.

Nothing really came to a head until I typed in Baltic States, here under Latvia I found a very enthusiastic young lady, called Lludmila. We corresponded very often, sometimes twice each week. She said that she had always been interested in Australia, especially Western Australia, and had read a lot of literature on it. She said that pictures of the outback was so different to her country, and she was longing to ride a horse and go swimming in a real ocean, in real hot weather.

I must admit that I embellished the stories I wrote up a bit. She was enthralled that you could drive for days on end without finding water, or people. She became very keen on coming out to Perth, and could I help her with the fare? For the second time in my life I fell for the pea and thimble trick. I replied that I would consider it was an honour to help her with the fare out here and yes she could stay with me in my house in Victoria Park. Also I still owned a house in Kalgoorlie. She sent me a photo of herself. She certainly was very curvaceous in her bikini. She looked about twenty five years of age, long blond hair extending half way down her back, thin ankles, nice long fingers, broad smile, and shiny teeth.

All in all, she seemed the real thing, and for a second time in my life I was really smitten. I put her photo in a frame and pinned it to the wall in the kitchen, so that when I did the dishes, I could look at it and go off in some sort of dream like state, thinking of the things we could do together. She spoke perfect English, no suggestion of an accent, said that she had studied it for years, first at Primary School, then at High School, and later when she did a Tourism Course, also she said that the whole family spoke English at home.

So what did I have to worry about? It all seemed all too easy and simple. However I learned that to sponsor a person out to Australia, required filling in reams of forms, and ticking the box which said was I going to marry her. I mused over this line for all of five seconds, and then ticked yes, sight unseen.

Oh boy, I had no idea what I was getting myself into. I was being swept along by a euphoria which was all consuming, and so I sent her most of the fare for the long plane trip out. Then, only after she had received the money that her emails got fewer and fewer apart. She started to make all sorts of excuses, firstly she had to go to hospital, for a week or two, then her father was dying and she couldn't come out at that time. So I waited and waited and was rapidly assuming that I had backed the wrong horse and lost all my money.

So the weeks of waiting turned into months, until one day after I had restarted back at the mine at Leinster, as the First Aid Officer, an email arrived saying that she was now free to arrange the flight. There I was back in cuckoo land, all agitated, went out the same day and bought some new shirts, pants, tie and jacket. I was delirious with the prospect of sharing my bed with such a bonza looking young woman. She never asked for more money, so all thoughts I had of being conned melted away. Wow! she was soon to be on the way, I was drunk with expectation.

Time seemed now to stand still. It seemed an age before I received the final email that she was leaving from the International airport at the capital Riga. Her brother Olav would drive her from their village Morupe, in his taxi, over the Daugava River, to the airport. From her previous emails, I gathered that she had two brothers and two sisters, she had given me their names but I have misplaced the copy of the email and have now forgotten them.

It was a Wednesday afternoon when her plane finally arrived at Perth International Airport. Doug had agreed I should have special leave. So I dressed up in my new cream shirt, red tie and jacket. I greased my hair down with Vaseline, shaved my stubble, put on some perfume and found a clean handkerchief. I was so nervous that I perspired all over. The plane was half an hour late, any longer and I would have fainted.

A huge Jumbo jet floated into view. The sun gleamed on the wings as it turned slowly to align itself with the runway, descended gracefully with its lights on and touched down on the tarmac without scattering the pigeons grazing on the grass alongside. The cabin door opened, passengers started to walk out. I couldn't pick out the youngish Ludmilla, so I went down stairs to the baggage pickup. The crowd thinned out. There were only fifty or so people left.

A plump woman about forty years old approached me. "Villian, vai tas esi tu?" she croaked, holding out her hand. I was shattered. "So sorrlie, I speak now in English, are you Villiam? "Yes I am," I stammered. "Esmu Ludmilla" My God, I saw my whole life flash before me, what have I done this time. What a botch-up, she can't speak English, she's not a blonde and she is about four stone heavier that I had expected. Her ankles were like an elephant. "es sagaidiju jaunnaku virieti, I vos expecting a younger man" she offered.

If I had a gun I would have gladly ended my life in the baggage section of the airport at that time. I had a wet shirt, and wet palms. My pulse would have been over the machine. God only would have known what my blood pressure was. I paled visibly. She wasn't too happy with me either. I was devastated, and started speaking pigeon English, "you have good flight?" I grunted, "you like coffee now?" I was a changed man, I was an idiot walking. I turned away smiling and shuffled toward the exit, pulling her over weight luggage, while she shuffled along behind me, in slippers muttering incomprehensible incantations, probably in Latvian. I was immune to all external sounds, I kept on walking, like a dead man trying to avoid his coffin.

"És riuniu druski latviski loerti lobbi" I muttered back between clenched teeth. It was the one of several sentences I had learned from the lady in the greengrocers shop around the corner to my house in Victoria Park. "vinch eir un skyiza maitena" I growled back, but alas my voice was muffled by the roar of the taxis starting their engines when they saw us coming. God Save the King used to be our National Anthem, pray God, save me now, resounded in my dull brain over and over, until we pulled up at the house, in Vic Park.

That night after dinner of sausages and mash, I said that I was going to take a shower. She came into the bathroom before I had time to lock the door. " I give you soap for shower "she said, and quickly she got to work, until I was covered in foam, even up to my mouth. All sensitivities were washed away in the foamy water. I did not return the favour. Later when she had had her shower, she came into the kitchen whilst I was doing the dishes and pondering over how I was going to handle the situation.

She immediately saw the photo that I had framed and had hung on the wall. She screamed and covered her mouth with her hand. "Ah, that is my little sister" she screamed, "vot is it doink here, how did you get it?" she queried. "I thought you had sent it to me" I replied. "no it vos not me, my little sister wrote those emails for me, ve all thought that it vos good fun, and make good laughs" That explained a lot for me. I saw it all. I had been taken for a sucker, and indeed I was. Had I known what the Chinese Philosopher had said all those years ago maybe I would have been more careful, who knows. I dried my hands, took out a bottle from the fridge, and passed into oblivion.

In the morning I realised just what it meant for the family back in Morupa to send their big sister out to Australia, hoping to get married. She had several sensuous night dresses, lots of very expensive perfume, together with shampoos and soaps. She wasn't the Latvian goddess that I had hoped to have, but she was a really nice person, and I felt very sorry for all the family. They were quite poor, everywhere in the countryside work was very difficult to obtain. Olav, her brother, was the best money earner for the whole family, and I respected him for that. It seems that their father, who was working as a waiter, in a case of mistaken identity, was bashed by foreigners, until he was pulp and died outside the restaurant, on the footpath, only a couple of years before.

Ludmilla was very keen to further our relationship. She seemed happy, particularly when I allowed her to use my computer in order to send home reports on how she was enjoying herself. After a month or so and a liberal supply of whiskey, the liaison was consummated. This was immediately conveyed to the family via email, to their great happiness. They sent us photos of the family seated around a large table, celebrating, with glasses raised, huge smiles, and silent best wishes.

In the darkness of our room, I felt her bare stomach. It was roughened, as if recently stretched. I asked her about it and was told that the reason why she had delayed in getting a flight was because she had had a baby whom she now had given to her sister, in order to come out here. As we showered together often, I had lots of opportunity to see the purple pregnancy stretch marks on her belly, the darkish stain around her nipples, and the previously swollen breasts now subsiding. I was glad the baby had arrived before she got to Perth.

I introduced her to the lady from the green grocer's shop. They met often and were happy to converse in Latvian. My vocabulary never improved. She came with me to Kalgoorlie by train, enjoying every minute of the trip, as it was so unique and like something out of another era. In the month that I was away in Leister, she had got a job as a bar lady in one of the pubs that line Hannon Street, and she was well liked. She seemed to have an ample amount of money. I very soon learned that she was skilled at making money from interested male "friends." I thought about it but didn't make the same mistake as I had before. I think that I had matured, and I wasn't prepared to start WW3. She even offered to repay me some of the money I had sent her. I felt I had no need to do that. So that's how we lived for the first year. Then she decided to leave me. She explained that under Australian law, all she had to do was to cohabit for a year, then she was able to take me to court and ask for half of all my assets. I was dumbfounded. I couldn't sleep. I took to the bottle again. I emailed her sister to tell her what Ludmilla was planning to do to me, but she said that it what the family had planned to do all along. Ludmilla had had three husbands, all marriages failed. She had two children, a boy and a girl. She applied for and received an Australian citizenship and got it, then an Australian Passport, and again got it without any problems, no questions asked. That was how things worked at that time.

So after a year, she left me and moved permanently to Kalgoorlie and opened a business for the pleasures of men. Pleasures from Abroad, I think it was called. I never visited there ever. From the gossip I heard that she was doing really well. She had done me for half of my money, and I was unable to do anything about it. The law was in her favour all the way. She was going to profit from my stupidity, and she now was able to call herself an Aussie. What a laugh!

I was left to pick up the pieces. I contacted the Department of Immigration and was told that this was happening all the time, with women entering the country from all over the world, on promises of a sham marriage, and as yet they didn't have all the answers to the problem, so I was out of luck as well as money.

I was having pains in my legs, so I visited my local doctor. The elder one was still away, having extended leave, so I saw the younger one for the second time." What's your problem now?" he asked. "Well" I replied, I have had pains in my Gastrocnemius, and I am worried." "hell what's that? " he came back. "it's the muscle in my calf" I said "Never did anatomy, at my university, was too hard, but I now regret it, and I am doing a course at night time. What was the name of that muscle again? And how do you know about it?"

So I had to tell him again that I had successfully completed a First Aid Course at St John's and received a handsome certificate, of which I was very proud. It seems that is the only thing I have ever done and not mucked it up somehow. He slid off his chair, and felt my leg. "does it hurt?" he said. "no" was the reply. "nothing wrong really" he said, "just take some Panadol, and you will be OK, by the way how is that thing you had on your Willie?" "It went away just as you said it would doctor, but then I had a rash on my belly, colour of bacon it looked like, but that went as well and so far, except for my leg I feel fine, thank you doctor" he smiled, wrote something on a piece of paper, "here hand this to the Receptionist, and see me again if it also doesn't go away, and that was that. However the pain persisted, so I went to another doctor when I was in Kalgoorlie, he said I had a Baker's cyst, at the back of my knee and that I needed an operation, pretty soon.

I waited a few weeks before a surgeon from Perth visited Kalgoorlie, and was told that I did not require surgery, but an Osmo patch put behind the knee each night, discarded in the morning until the swelling had subsided. I told him I had seen another doctor in Perth, but he didn't pick up any swelling. Also he had never done anatomy. "some mickey mouse university," I suppose, the surgeon replied "some students refuse to attend lectures nowadays, think they can study better by themselves, no need to get out of bed at all, it's a changing world alright." he said slowly and somewhat sadly. "Tell me about it " I said, smiling thoughtfully, before I turned toward the door, and left.

CHAPTER 4

Third Time Lucky

A LONG TIME AFTER these events, my foot started to give me heaps of trouble again, the pain was so bad, that I couldn't sleep at all. I had taken all the pain killers I had in the house, so I took to the heavy stuff again. It had no benefit at all, so caught a taxi out to the Kalgoorlie Hospital. Lucky for me there was a visiting orthopaedic surgeon, and he saw me almost right away. He squeezed my foot sideways, backwards, pulled on my toes until I yelled in agony, and then said ruefully, that I needed another operation. According to him, I had a Morton's neuroma. The nerves in my foot had become embroiled in the healing of the broken bones and had to be sorted out. Doug wasn't happy, as he said, he couldn't do much about it and I had better go back onto compo.

And so I did. Looking after myself was quite hard. After the operation, again I had to bear a heavy plaster on my left ankle, which meant that walking was hard even using a stick or a crutch. It looked as though I didn't have much choice but to buy an electric chair from the chemist at the Hospital. This proved to be a Godsend, and I was able to navigate around the house, even to the closest shopping centre. In the afternoons I relaxed on the veranda, reading Shakespeare, and some poems, which my neighbour had loaned me, or books which I got from the local library.

One sunny afternoon, I heard the creak of the Iron Gate in the middle of the front fence, and through the filtered sunlight coming between the leaves of a large kumquat tree that covered part of the veranda, I saw a young nurse walking up the broken pathway that led to the front door. Quickly she spied me, turned to the right, and addressed me "Bill, my name is Elaine Woodbridge, I am a Silver Chain Nurse, and I have been asked by the Hospital to visit you, just to confirm that you are coping, being all alone.

I was really startled, and so it was a little while before I had collected my thoughts and answered her. "That's so kind of you Elaine, I had no idea that the Silver Chain did home visits, as I was about to make a cuppa, would you care to join me?" "Yes I would love to" she replied, "But only if I could make it" "that's fine" I answered, " you will find everything ready in the kitchen, plus some Xmas cake in a Mills and Ware's red tin on the bench. There's a black tom- cat meowing near the back door. Take no notice of him, he's a damn nuisance, belongs next door. Please don't feed him anything,- please!"

Soon she reappeared, with a tray, a fresh pot of piping hot tea, and a handsome serve of cake, all under a net to deter the ever present flies. We sat in the fading sun light on the veranda, slurping our tea and talking about almost anything. Elaine was both a good listener and a good talker. She had been well educated at a high school in Perth. She also acted in the local repertory club.

When the best of the sunshine had passed, we went inside to the sitting room. Here she saw the piano I had sent up from the house in Victoria Park. I don't play, I'm not clever enough, but I know that others might like to do so. She sat down, adjusted the stool height, flexed her fingers, and then started to play, no sheet music, just memory. Beethoven was her favourite, her repertoire included Handel, Brahms and Chopin. What a delight I was treated to, for over half an hour. Then she realised that she had to ride her bicycle home to prepare a meal for her elderly aunt, with whom she was living. She found enough time to give me a haircut. Then she was off but called out to say that she would return tomorrow.

When she left, part of me went too. I became agitated from anticipation. Next morning I rose early, shaved, and got myself dressed in my new clothes, cream shirt, red tie, and jacket. Maybe it was going a bit overboard, but who cares? It was a chance to make a good impression, and I was going for it. All night I thought about her. Clearly I saw her face before me. Her hair was pulled back from her face, and tied in a bun. It was brownish and smooth, her skin was lightly tanned and soft, her eyes were almond shaped, her voice soft and warm. She was indeed a very warm hearted young lady, and it was of no concern if I stayed in this plaster for a whole year, as long as she could come and see me every day. What talent she had. Played the piano, sang and acted in plays. I had none of these skills,

Each day she looked at my left foot. There was a piece of wire sticking out from my fourth toe. Each day she tweaked it, each day it hurt a lot. I tried very hard not to appear a wimp, but I just couldn't help it. It was only after three months that I was able to stand her pulling on the wire a little bit each day, further and further out from my fourth toe. Finally one day she said "now Bill, be brave, this is the day we have been waiting for. I think your bones have now knitted together. Hold on to the arm of your chair and pull!" The wire after a slow start slid out. There was a little bit of blood, but the pain wasn't as bad as I expected. "well done! "She cried out and came forward and kissed me on my right cheek. "you can probably get rid of the plaster inside a month, Bill" She was clearly pleased, and soon rode off on her bicycle, singing Advance Australia Fair. I watched her ride down the road, turn the corner near the greengrocer and disappear from sight.

In about a month she arranged for me to go to hospital and have the plaster removed. It was a huge relief, and each day my walking improved. Each day she helped me walk to the veranda, and we practised dancing, slowly at first, then circles and jives. One day I held her so closely. I could feel her heart beat, she laid her head on my shoulder, and we entered a world of bliss. I kissed her head, and said how much I thanked her for her encouragement and professional dedication. I said I couldn't do without her and she could come and stay permanently with me, anytime.

She lifted her head and in a soft voice whispered she had fallen in love with me. It was I who had encouraged her, she said. "I knew there was something between us, from the very first moment we met, and I would like nothing more than to live with you, but I have an elderly aunt to look after. She is all I have from our family. I promised my mother, before she passed away, last year, that I would look after her sister as long as she needed me, and I cannot break that promise. And I have also made a promise that I will help the disadvantaged here in Kalgoorlie, where I was born, as long as I am able. I must put these two vows above my own personal desires."

She was a Saint without doubt. I cuddled her even more closely, tears fell down my cheeks and wet her coloured frock, what had I done to deserve this, I thought. I could never be called a Saint, so why was it? I never found out the answers, but simply accepted what life threw up to me. Each day I spent time with her, I still needed a crutch, so I was still on compo. Late each afternoon we sat and talked in the sitting room. We started a file, planning our wedding. There was a lot to do, caterers, church, venue, best man, speeches, grog. We had them all listed and taken care of.

Doug rang and said that I could start back at Leinster as the First Aid man just as soon as I was fit enough. I had to be able to run twenty yards, and walk over a hundred yards, before I was deemed to have regained my fitness. I was almost there, anyway I now needed the extra money, as my bank account was down to its lowest ever.

It was difficult to get used to after so long away. The other miners annoyed me too, as they were so dim and dumb. They weren't safety conscious, so I feared that someday there would be a serious accident. I implemented a series of accident training exercises, so that each man knew his duty, if needed. The group acted as if I was over cautious, as no harm was ever going to come to them. I despaired.

Within the next six months we had two rock falls. The first put no one in danger, but the second crushed one man, killing him, and seriously injured another. The safety alarm screamed. All the men jumped to it, at the double. Each knew just what to do. They cleared the scene in record time. They gave CPR to the injured man, bandaged him on the spot, and had him on a stretcher quicker than we had ever practised. I was so proud of the boys, and was congratulated by Doug when I returned to Kalgoorlie.

When I saw Elaine again, she said that her aunty now had pneumonia, and may not last very long. We had been together for over eighteen months, I think. I am not too good when it comes to money or time. One day is so much like any other, it is for me anyway all too difficult. Life for me just seems to float on and on. One day whilst I was on this leave, Elaine rode her bike over to tell me that her aunty had passed away that morning, and she would be occupied organising the funeral. I went out the front door to see her off. The sun was well over the yardarm and visibility was a bit hazy from the dust that gets blown around almost each afternoon in Kalgoorlie. The last thing I called to her was to be careful riding her bike on the way home, "there are lots a half drunks around" I yelled after her. I watched her approach the corner. She seemed to wobble a little. She had seen a dump truck coming too fast up on her right hand side. She had her left leg down to slow herself, but she fumbled and went underneath the giant left hand wheel. She was gone in a flash. The truck took fifty yards to stop. People came out of their houses, since they had heard the noise. I was struck dumb.

The Police arrived, I made a statement, Zigowski the driver was charged. He was over twice the limit. He served five years. Sadly I had to organise two funerals, to be held together, in a week's time. Nurses came from the Silver Chain Office, and formed a guard of honour at the church front door, as did members of the Repertory Club. Doug and some of my team came from the mine leaving only a skeleton staff. The service was conducted by the Rev. John Cartwright, who only a short time ago had officiated at the crushed miner's funeral.

It was the hottest part of summer, but although Kalgoorlie had absolutely no flowers, the wreath I received was perfect. Made up of Elaine's favourite flowers, red and white roses. I gave the eulogy, and broke down twice, said I had never met her aunty, but for me Elaine was a Saint, and described just how she singlehandedly guided me back, from an abyss to the reality of a future life. As well as my Dad, she was my soul mate. We then departed to the cemetery. The two graves were side by side, close to that of her parents. She had upheld the vows she had made and I have absolutely no doubt she will be rewarded in Heaven.

She had so much to live for, her music, her acting, her dedication to the disadvantaged. She was about thirty five years old and childless. Her memory has remained with me over the years. I never ever met another woman, I didn't need to, since Elaine was always with me, in my dreams, at work in the mines, at home bent over a hot stove, cooking or washing up. "The music in my heart I bore, long after it was heard no more" (William Wordsworth [1770-1850] The Reaper)

CHAPTER 5

The Aftermath

THE EFFECT OF ELAINE'S accident had a profound effect on me. I took special leave again and returned to the house in Victoria Park. It brought back so many black memories of my stupidity that I was unhappy and morose. It was impossible to live there anymore, so I arranged to have it sold. Of course I lost money. When does one sell anything and actually gain something. Very rarely, I think, certainly it was never my experience, however I received a modest price and with that I bought a slightly smaller house in Star St Carlisle, and still had a little over.

This house was obviously built for a single person. All the rooms were only about two thirds the size of those in Vic Park. They were cold and damp, the shower and bathroom had been added on to the back of the house, as an afterthought. The kitchen was in the middle and overlooked the neighbour, so I had a blind installed. The dining room was pathetic, There was only a small table set in the centre of the room under a faded lamp shade and a forty watt globe. I wrote a list of things to have repaired but was in no hurry to go ahead and spend more money. So I vacillated and waited.

The sitting room could only accommodate one other person, and it had an unpleasant smell, as if the previous owner or person who may have rented the house, may have had a dog, or two. I tried to fumigate the couch and the three cushions, but that was only partially successful, so I dragged it all onto the back lawn and set it on fire. The local Brigade wasn't impressed with me. When they saw the smoke they thought they had a real doozie on their hands, so turned out in force, only to find it was a fizzer on the back lawn.

One thing the house did have was a telephone, and one day Doug actually tracked me down and asked how long more did I need to take off from the mine. He told me quite bluntly that if my problems were psychological, then don't even think of returning. "We've got too many fruit cakes here already, we don't want any more" he retorted. I thought about this. Maybe my problems were actually in my mind, so I rang him back and told him that I would report for duty just as quickly as I could. But my heart wasn't in it. I had been a miner for all of my life. Sure I had a lot of time off from the constant fear of an accident, or serious injury, but I had also had a lot of problems to deal with, and I lived in constant dread of getting depression again. A dark cloud hovers just above your head, just out of reach of grabbing it with both hands, and strangling it. It pervades your whole life from the arrival of the warm glow over the hills each morning, until you hit the pillow and ask God to help you gain some sleep that night.

When I lived with a lady friend, I wasn't too bad, but it never really leaves you alone. It's there ready to attack when you are by yourself and down a bit. Alcohol is not the answer, it never has been, and in my case it seemed to make the depression worse. Women suffer from it just as do men of all ages. Since my mother had it, I wonder if is hereditary. Who knows? Who cares?

My team of bearded blokes welcomed me back, patting me on the back and calling me "Champ" Some said they really missed me and could we start some exercises again? But I wasn't the same person that I had been when Elaine was with me. Now I was older, slower and lacked interest in most things. Some of the blokes said they wanted me to join the dart group at the local. No need to drink Hannan's Larger all the time, the team captain, Jason was also a teetotaller. I shook my head, I just wasn't interested.

I was now getting the odd headache. It was difficult to be specific about it. Sometimes it felt as if it was in the middle of my head, other times in the front, and then it could be on one side or the other, so I didn't report it, especially as I don't think Doug would have given me any more time off. A really good friend, Curley, asked me to come with him on a Friday night to see the new types of barmaid in some of the pubs, in Hannon's street. They're called skimpy's and sometimes they only wear just a big smile. Sales at all the hotels have gone up over five hundred percent, he urged.

But his pleading was to no avail. He got really cross with me. "What's the trouble mate?" he asked "are you sick or something?" "I don't really know Curley" I replied "I think that I have something going on in my head, but don't know just what" he lost interest and faded away bewildered. So my popularity was dropping and I couldn't do anything about it. I lasted probably another five years, I'm not sure. I drifted, as if in a haze. Some days I was reasonably alert and jovial, other days I was back to being really bad company to be with. However I tried and tried to be on good terms with my group. I even joined the dart group, just to show that I wasn't a wimp at all. At first my aim wasn't too bad, I would score at least twenty or more, slowly I noticed it was deteriorating, now I couldn't see the bullseye clearly so fudged it and just imagined where it might be. At least I didn't hit anybody, the side wall yes, but no real damage to any person.

Later the headaches evolved into attacks of giddiness. I stumbled a lot, and walked with a wide gait. It wasn't possible to use a walking stick whilst working on the mines, you would look so stupid. So I kept going, smiled a lot at anyone and everyone, tried to be the big fella, by laughing loudly at times especially at lunch time in the mess, so that my mates started looking at me suspiciously.

Soon I was asked to have a talk with Doug in his office. "There has been a lot of people complaining about you Bill," he said as I entered the painted door to his office, "Well, what the bloody hell is it all that about?" I yelled at him "What the fuck is it their business?" I continued "Dull bastards all of them, lazy dull bastards, sack the lot of them, I would." I shouted.

Doug, who had been a real friend to me in the past, stood up and came round to my side of his desk. He took me by the shoulders. "Bill," he said calmly, "You have never shouted at me ever before, what's the matter? Aren't you well? Are you feeding yourself properly? Unfortunately Bill, because of the safety around a mine site, I must ask you to leave, and soon please, everyone is worried about you. Please get help. Pick up your pay tomorrow about lunch time. I will present you with something then. I will address the men." He hugged me tightly. I could feel his tears running down my cheek. We broke free, I turned and walked towards the door. "Tomorrow, then, at noon? I asked quietly "at noon" came the reply "Thank you, so much" I muttered, as I opened the door and slinked away down the few steps and onto the gravel path that led to the front gate and anonymity. I didn't want to attend the meeting, but I made myself. I got up early, showered, shaved and dressed myself in my cream shirt, red tie and jacket. Because my hands were a bit shaky I cut myself just under my chin, so I put a tissue on it until it stopped bleeding. Twelve o'clock arrived, I walked proudly into the mess hall. It was full with miners who had just completed their first shift of the day.

As I entered, they all rose as one and cheered long and loud. Doug was there. He held his hands up to gain some silence, but had to wait, until the noise abated. "Gentlemen, this is indeed a sad moment" more loud cheers. "Bill, is leaving us today. We have been together for over twenty years. He worked his first five years without taking leave. Then he had an accident, and was away for over a year. We all missed him during that time. He had broken his foot bones and this has caused him lots of trouble. It is a credit to him that he returned at all, but he did as the First Aid Officer that you know so well. (more cheers)

I am sure that many of you owe your lives to this extraordinary man, Bill Dunbar, his name will soon be added to our Board of Honour, that hangs over there near the billiard table. For me it has been a privilege to have worked with him and I wish him all the very best for his retirement, on behalf of the Governors I would like to present Bill with this small memento, as a reward for his long and devoted service to this Company." At that he turned, shook hands, and presented me with a gold watch, to attach to my fob pocket. He gestured that I should reply. I stepped forward, never having made a speech before.

"Friends," I started, maybe a little nervous, "I loves youse all" All one hundred and fifty of them rose and cheered, then they broke out singing "For he's a jolly good fellow" as they carried me on their shoulders twice around the room. What better Aussie farewell could I have had? A few handshakes, and I was out the door and into a Company vehicle to take me to the station. My life as a miner had come to a sudden end. At the station I waved to the driver who had brought me until the steam from the engine erased all sign of life on the platform. I was again alone in the cabin, with only my memories and thoughts, as the train rocked and rolled its way toward Perth.

CHAPTER 6

Pennington House

AFTER I SAW THE eye specialist last Thursday I have been seriously thinking that I may need to be admitted to some kind of nursing home, where they provide three meals a day, can offer help with showering, shaving and getting dressed. Maybe I could be lucky and be helped by someone like Elaine, but I doubt it. Saints don't come along in one's life that often. My sight has now dropped off considerably, and I am nervous and insecure. Driving is now out of the question, so I have locked the utility up securely, covered it with a tarpaulin, for protection against the rain and the summer heat and of course bird droppings. I gave her a gentle pat on the side door. She had been a true and faithful friend, and so I said my goodbyes. My future was now uncertain. I am at the whim of the Gods.

As I have explained in the Prologue, I saw in the morning paper a small add about an old folks home called Pennington House. It was situated in the country a few miles from Katanning, I assumed that it had been an old farm, so I dialled the phone number. I held on and on, redialled again several times, but to no avail. I reread the advertisement over and over, wrote out the phone number in three letter groups so that I wasn't missing anything out, and tried again. I phoned a Real estate agent in Kalgoorlie and asked him to put my house there up for sale. He replied that sales in Kalgoorlie at that moment were dead in the water, so I phoned Doug and told him that I was sending all the papers to him and that the Company could use it for sick miners, if they wanted to. He thanked me and wished me all the best. He seemed distant and aloof.

I vacillated for about an hour, then made a decision to get on a bus and go down to Katanning and have a look at Pennington House first hand. The bus left from the railway station in Wellington Street, opposite to the Mines Department, just after ten o'clock. There were only five or six passengers on board when we took off. We headed out to York. There were sheep and wheat farms everywhere. Despite my poor eyesight, the whole countryside seemed dry and dead, there were no pastures that one might expect. I wondered what might lie ahead. Beverley looked worse, then Brookton and on to Pingelly before arriving at Katanning. I was the last passenger to alight. The main Street was deadly quiet, a stray dog yelped in the distance. I went into a small café, sat down on a dusty chair and ordered a coffee, no they did not do a cappuccino, so called after the Capuchin Franciscan monks in Italy, who had bald heads, white cassocks and brown habits. Looking down on the mug the resemblance was quite real. What type of coffee did they make I enquired, only instant, I'm afraid came the reply, there's just not the people, there used to be around here, the waitress said, just the odd farmer coming to town for supplies, sometimes we go for days without serving a coffee.

She looked to be about twenty two years old. I wondered just what her future may be. I asked if I could get a taxi out to Pennington House. Don't know really, she replied. "Old George Jones used to have a taxi, but I think he has closed down, wait while I ring him" she said. So I waited on the footpath, and I waited, probably for about twenty five minutes. She came out to tell me that she had "no luck, he could be anywhere, try the pub, only two blocks away, and he goes there for lunch. He had come out as a migrant from Germany, changed his name, probably trying to escape from a Fraulein or the law".

So I dragged my bag the two blocks, saw the local, went inside and found George easily because he was the only one there. He was scoffing a pint while munching on a sandwich. He would have been about seventy, his arms were weather beaten, his face like a piece of dried leather, his finger nails needed attention, and he had bruises on his elbows. He had no teeth. I don't think he was too fit, but who knows, old gnarled gum trees can live for ever, and so George may just be one like that.

"Sit and have a pint and a sandwich" he mumbled to me, so I did, all very enjoyable. "Now pay me the money, it will cost ya twenty five quid" he requested," I need the money to fill er up " he said. I followed him along the windswept footpath for a couple of blocks until we found his taxi. Frankly I don't think it would have met the requirements for registration, but this was Katanning and who cares? We drove the bone shaker to the garage and filled her up, then we headed out beyond the tree line into the open plain of sheep farming country. Here, there hadn't been a good soaking rain for years. It was impossible to talk to George because of the noise the old girl made over the rough roads, but we arrived in one piece, after half an hour. He stopped about a quarter of a mile short of the front gate, George refused to go any closer. He shouted "Raus mit euch, Danke schon" which I took to mean, "Get out", so I did. He had some fear about the place. I asked for a refund, but the wily old bird smiled, wiped his hand across his sagging gums, laughed quietly and said "no way mate", and I could see that he was fair dinkum, inexorably so, so I didn't persist, but grabbed my bag, thanked him, and strode off to find out what was behind the little fence. There was a slight rise in the road, so I was puffing when I got to the gate. This was tied fast, obviously to stop someone getting out and taking off, so I just lifted my leg and got over it.

Pennington House was impressive when seen from the front gate, as it stood on a slight mound. It was made completely of wood, it was tall, because it had two stories and an attic. All the windows had curtains behind them. I trudged up the gravel path pulling my bag of a few possessions. I knocked on the front door, but got no response. I rang the bell, but I don't think it had been connected to a power source for years.

So I walked around the left side of the house, trying to find a back entrance. The door, which was only a flimsy flywire was open so I walked in to a largish kitchen. I shouted to attract attention, and then I heard a noise. It was a man arguing with a woman, who soon appeared. The woman seemed distraught. The man saw me and called "Hi, I'm Wally and this is my wife Bev. Every day she is lugubrious since she has lost her memory, doesn't know me and won't let me help her. We fight all the time, if you are looking for Charlie, I think you will find him in the shed out the back." He seemed quite a kindly avuncular gentleman but under pressure.

I retraced my steps back to the flimsy flywire, and out to the back yard. On the right hand side there was a broken down wooden shed. As I approached I heard a click. I well knew the sound of that click, so I started hurrying until I came to the entrance. Looking inside, the sunlight made it difficult to see anything clearly, but over against a bench was a tallish thin man pushing the barrels of a shotgun down his throat. He wasn't able to get his fingers on to the trigger, fortunately. I shouted to him, clapped my hands together, grabbed a tin can, dropped it, all to distract him from what he was trying to achieve. Although I was shaking, I managed to shout out "Good God man just what are you doing?" That must have done it, as he pulled the barrels from his mouth, placed the gun onto the bench and said with some asperity "who the hell are you?" He seemed really curmudgeonly type of person. I told him my story, and he approached and shook hands. "Gets a bit lonely round here, my wife has left me, I can't cope by myself, so I thought I would end it all."

Behind him attached to the wall were two faded black and white photos. On the left were four airmen standing in front of a Wellington Bomber. The right hand photo was of a wreck, probably the Bomber after a crash landing. Wally told me later that the two pilots on the left of the photo were Charles's brothers. In 1940 they left their home in Hamilton NZ and joined the RAF. None returned. They were strafed after bombing the German submarine base. Lost the landing gear, ran out of fuel just four miles short of Henley airport, crash landed, skidded and hit a wall. The two brothers, although still alive, died of their injuries in hospital two weeks later.

"Let's have a cuppa" I said confidently. And so we did, after walking back from the shed and into the kitchen. Wally had beaten us and had the pot boiling on the gas stove.

The three of us sat around the kitchen table. When Charlie shuffled away to get a second cup, I whispered to Wally, what had happened in the shed. He told me that it happened regularly. Charles wasn't married, but he thought he was, to Muriel the house keeper, who was away seeing the doctor, then collecting the stores for the next week. According to Wally, who seemed to have his finger on the pulse around here, Muriel was having crippling pains in her belly, at regular intervals, at least every month, and after a few months, she was now quite worried, lest she had cancer.

"Bit dry around here, Charles" I said, inanely, when he returned with his second cuppa. "My God it is, haven't seen the rain for years now," he replied sitting down on another chair to the one he had been using. I thought that he also, was losing his marbles. "I haven't got the money to pay the bills now" he said sadly, "that's why my wife and I opened this place up as a nursing home, some time ago, but we have only had two people come here, Wally and Bev, nice folk, quiet, but they don't play scrabble anymore."

"Charles I have some money, which I don't really need, and you and Muriel can use it to pay off the debts." I offered. "She's gone bush" he replied, "don't know why, maybe she's after some young fella in the town, bugger, she should have told me she was going, damn her, now what are you talking about?."

Charles came and sat alongside me. He was a tall man, about six feet four. He had a largish head and jaw. His whitish hair was thinning especially across his forehead. The skin of his head was pale, since he had always worn a large brimmed hat when outdoors and he had avoided sunburn to his scalp. However his face was tanned, as were his arms. He had a small lump on the side of his nose, and several areas of roughness on his arms. His hands were like spades, huge, and gnarled by time and weather. He told me that he was born in Hamilton, New Zealand and had migrated to Australia when the economy there took a nose dive, about twenty years ago. When he came to this area around Katanning, the pasture was lush and the property carried nearly a sheep per acre, not bad for Australia, but no way near what they can carry in NZ, which can be as high as fifteen an acre when the season is good.

"Did you know that in the south island they do bloat patrols each night." "No what's that," I enquired "well cattle form gas in their rumen, when the Lucerne or the clover is too rich. The left side of their abdomen swells up, and they go down. Now if you don't get to them real quick and punch a knife into their belly, two fingers below the rib cage, and let out the gas, they will die, and you can't afford that to happen. I did that for years before I came over here. Never heard of it happening in Australia," he said as he shook his head. "Can't anything be done to prevent this" I enquired?

"Yes of course it can" he retorted "you can spray kerosene onto the pasture, if you have the money, keeps the gas from forming, so that the cattle can burp, and they don't develop that swelling on their left side." There doesn't seem much wrong with his distant memory, I thought just his recent memory, and like what has happened this morning, where was Muriel. Talking to Charles puzzled me. At times his voice became quite orotund. I'm sure that I had read something about this condition, in a magazine somewhere, or was it in those First Aid lesions? After a while it dawned on me "Oh, yes, it's presbyophrenia, I shouted out to anyone within earshot.

And there was, Wally. He heard me and came rushing into the kitchen. "are you talking about Charles?" he queried "yes, yes" I replied, "are you sure that it's not Korsakoff's?" he came back, "well has he been a serious drinker?" I replied, "never heard him or Muriel mention it," Wally answered. After I questioned him about this, he told me that he had at some stage in his life been a psychiatric nurse at Grayland's Hospital, but left after a patient bashed him up.

In the weeks that followed, Charles showed that he was disoriented, could never find things again such as his tools, which he left in the house or on his bench in the shed and started talking rubbish, that is, confabulating, spooky stuff, and it helped to keep me awake at night. He flatly refused to wear his reading glasses.

That night it was really hot and my room quiet stuffy. I just couldn't get to sleep after about 2 am, so I got up, crept as quietly as I could down the creaky spiral staircase, holding tightly onto the banister, and so into the kitchen, where I made a cup of tea. I tiptoed through the flimsy flywire door and into cooler air outside. To my surprise Charles was also there, sitting alone and looking up at the stars, rhythmically tapping his brogues on the wooden floor of the veranda.

"Hi Charles" I half whispered. "What are you doing here?" he inquired, as I pulled up an old wicker chair and sat next to him. "Do you fear death, Bill?" he queried. "Haven't thought about it much" I replied, "I have" he muttered, "All my life I have been fascinated by what happens to us when our time is up on this earth. See those stars up there?" "Yes, Charles" I replied. "Well I reckon that you and I are heading for one of them pretty soon, to remain there until we are required to return to earth to spiritualise another human being." He paused for a long time, chewing on a biscuit or something.

"Bill," he continued," We are all destined to eventually leave this dystopian world, and be free from its squalor, terror, deprivation, oppression, disease, overcrowding, and pogroms.(another but shorter pause) I am convinced that our spirit will live on in a utopian state, for a change, on one of the stars. Don't forget that the mass-energy of the human spirit is irrepressible and cannot be destroyed, as Lavoisier had explained in 1789 in the Law of Conservation of Mass. It will survive in one form or another for millennia"

I sat slightly mesmerised for over an hour, listening intently to Charles's philosophy on life after death. I had never heard him so lucid, so purposeful, and so vociferous. He had always been a self-made man, like me, since he had left school in NZ, reading widely at every opportunity. That is the reason why he could talk on such a variety of subjects, at the dinner table, when the dishes had been removed, and particularly when he was having one of his better moments. I was overwhelmed by his fascinating exegesis.

I crept downstairs again looking for some cooler air, about two or three nights later. Charles had already taken up his place when I arrived and was muttering to himself and looking upwards towards the heavens, as I adjusted the cushion on the old wicker chair and sat next to him.

"They killed him you know" he offered "who killed who?" I enquired "the church, of course" came the terse reply. "The holy bloody Catholic church, they imprisoned him, starved him, beat him senseless until he died, but I know that he is up there looking down on us mortals. His day will come; triumphantly he will return to earth and again ride his white donkey, holding the golden cross of his High Office, high in the air for all to see" "Charles, I'm sorry, I just don't follow you, who are you referring to?" Charles turned slowly towards me, looked me straight in the eyes and said Peter Morrone of course, as if I was a complete dim wit. "Charles you must forgive me but who was Peter Morrone?

Charles sighed and cleared his throat a little, adjusted his kitchen chair in my direction, the dim light from an ascending moon shone meekly onto his aging face. He smiled at me and said, half in a whisper, "we have to go back to 1215, when Peter Angelerio was born to a peasant farming family in Iserna in Italy. He was the eleventh of twelve children, his father died when he was only six. He entered the Benedictine abbey for three years and was ordained a priest in Rome but there after he withdrew to Mount Morrone, above Salmona, to become a hermit, but gathering a group of monks around him wearing a white habit, black hood and a black mantle and calling themselves "The Morronese"

In 1294 Fra Pietro, after the papal coronation, caused by King Charles 11, interrupting the cardinal conclave and ordering them to hurry up and elect a new Pope, fearing that the Papacy would return to France, where it had been for eighty years; called himself Pope Celestine V. He lasted only about ten months and retired, having been forced from Office by Pope BonifaceV111. Since you just can't have two Popes, the Swiss guards chased him across the Apennines, finally, he was captured on the beach, by Guglielmo L'Estendard on the 16th May 1295, after his little boat was blown back to Italy during a storm in the Adriatic. He was made a prisoner in a freezing castle, out of sight, until he died, on the 19th May 1296, just one year and three days later." Charles, always the dilettante, then turned back to gazing upward, watching the twinkling stars with tears in his eyes. I left him there, peacefully in his own world and crept up the stairs and back to my bed, thankful of the encounter.

Muriel arrived back home after a day or two. She drove her utility almost up to the back door, tooted loudly, and called out for Charles or Wally to help her bring in the shopping. I responded to the call, she was bending over when I arrived, and when I said "Hi there" she jumped a little. "Blimey, who the heck are you?" she demanded. "Where are the two boys?" "don't really know, I haven't seen them for a few hours," I said, "but I'm Bill Dunbar, and I have already been here a few days. "I'm Muriel, I'm the house keeper, pleased to meet ya"

Now the house was filling up. Muriel was a real character, she was tall but not as tall as Charles. She was well built, well-muscled grizzled, but not unattractive. She had large bags under her eyes and a pigmented lesion on the right side of her neck. Charles was the first to arrive, he gave her a kiss on the cheek, but didn't seem to realise she had been away. Wally came, looking a bit groggy, I think he had been asleep, and was abruptly awoken by Muriel's ingress. However we all got to it and soon had the back of the utility cleared out and the goods placed in their correct spot in the kitchen.

She soon gave me another cup of tea, sat at the table, and asked me to tell her just why I chose to be here. I went through all the events leading up to my arrival. She listened carefully, asked some questions, and when I told her that she and Charles could have the fifty thousand pounds I had brought with me her whole attitude changed. She insisted that I know that she and Charles were definitely not married. Charles thinks so, she said, and I play along with it, but no we do not sleep together, no way, never have done and never will. "He's a nice fellow, but he has long since lost his marbles, only talks of New Zealand, and the sylvan countryside and of course of the number of sheep we used to have here."

That night I slept in a better bed upstairs, I was now a VIP, and she looked after me really well. I didn't mind, it wasn't difficult to take, in fact I revelled in a bit of TLC. It brought back memories of better times in my life, the real warmth of another human being. The fun of laughter, and good conversation. Charles was most of the time, dead meat, but I am sure we all adjusted to him, and structured our conversations accordingly. Muriel even got the box of scrabble down from the cupboard in the kitchen and we had a few games. Alas Wally and I got tired easily, me particularly, because I couldn't see too clearly, and it was a struggle to keep up, so I used to excuse myself and retire about nine o'clock. It took a long time to get the bed really warm on most nights, so I rubbed my feet together, until my left one let me know not to be too rough.

Over the following weeks Muriel and I had some very in depth, pragmatic discussions. I told her about the three ladies in my life, and she had some terse remarks to make about what twits men could be. Why had she never married? Or had she. I never found out as she would never disclose anything about herself, or her family, or even where she was born, was she too a New Zealander? I will never know, but she exuded a worldliness far beyond her years, I felt. We became such good friends, poor Wally was aging rapidly, with all the stress with his wife Bev. She even threatened him with a kitchen knife one day, yelling at him that her husband would be coming soon and would take care of poor old Wally, whom she didn't recognise. It was so sad for him to be subjected to all this humiliation, but he took it all in his stride and never hurt her in any way. He was a real Aussie bloke and a devoted husband.

As the days passed into weeks, my headaches were getting more frequent, and so were the attacks of giddiness. On some days my speech was slurred, and some words I just couldn't tackle at all. Words like slovenly, sober, solitude, solemnity, seems they all start with an S. Muriel was very helpful, "were all getting older" she used to say, laughing, as if there was nothing really to worry about, as she made up my bed, shaking the pillows vigorously.

Muriel was always most blithe in the mornings. She called her favourite birds, mainly magpies, to the back door, each day before breakfast, talked to them, and then threw them some scraps to enjoy. She also had a favourite black, slightly overweight, three legged male cat (after having lost his left rear leg in a rabbit trap) of obscure origin, with a missing front incisor tooth, whom she named Blackboy. This made calling him quite difficult, so sometimes we got "Blackie!", sometimes we got "Boy Boy!". Whatever, it usually did the trick, and Blackboy would emerge slowly from his feline world, just long enough for breakfast and of course a cuddle.

CHAPTER 7

Tea Leaves

ONE MORNING AFTER BREAKFAST, Muriel asked all of us, if we would be interested in having someone come out to Pennington House and talk to us after tea one evening. It really came down to Wally and myself, as Bev was always on another planet, Charles, always unreliable; some days he was lucid, at other times he was vague and unresponsive. Wally saw no reason to prevent it happening, I agreed, and so Muriel was instructed to organise these events.

After a few days, we all gathered after breakfast, for an update. Muriel explained that she had contacted a retired clairvoyant, living quietly in Busselton, who would be willing to come all the way over to PH, somewhere about seven in the evening, and was very willing to "read our cups" at no expense.

About a week later she failed to show up, but rang Muriel, explaining that her mode of transport had fallen through. It appears that a relative had agreed to pick her up and drive her over, however at the last minute, he cancelled, explaining that he had just lost his vehicle license on account of being over the limit for C2H5OH.

I actually overheard this telephone conversation. Muriel was very understanding and even offered to drive over to Busselton and pick her up, adding that she could stay the night, have breakfast with us, before Muriel would drive her back home in the morning. Thus the arrangements were agreed upon for the following week, which gave Muriel plenty of time to explain to us who this lady was and how she became a clairvoyant.

Her name was Madam Anatola Stringlet, she was very elderly, slightly hard of hearing, had a high pitched voice and was very intolerant of fools, sceptics and disbelievers. She had studied the lesions of the famous Polish clairvoyant Madame Blavatsky, and had established a very good name in the South West of Western Australia, where she had taught, held seminars, tutorials, picture slide evenings, and séances in the town halls, for many years.

About four in the afternoon, Muriel opened the front gate, climbed into the flattop, let the brake off, and rolled silently onto the road and headed toward Busselton. She arrived back, just after Sunset towards seven o'clock. We all had had dinner, and I was looking out of the window of my room, as Muriel revved up the drive way, stopping near the back door. I had a clear view of Madam Stringlet as she gingerly got out from the front seat of the flattop. Yes, she was very elderly, quite unsteady on her feet, dressed all in black, and was wearing a largish red scarf around her neck, she had the appearance of a true ascetic. Muriel quickly hustled her through the back door and went back to the flattop to get her suit case. I thought that I had seen another woman, but I am unsure.

An hour or so later, after I had negotiated the stairs and was waiting in the dining room for Wally and Bev to arrive, Muriel appeared and said that I could go first. Muriel went ahead to show me the smallish room off the dining room where Madam Stringlet had ensconced herself. Muriel tapped softly on the door, until a high pitched voice called out. "It's open." Muriel held the door ajar, and ushered me inside.

At first I couldn't see anything in the darkness, so I just stood still until Madam Stringlet whispered in a soft undertone that there was a chair right in front of me. "Do sit down, don't be frightened" Just what was it that I could have been frightened of, I wondered. Looking straight ahead I thought that I could just make out a table and some sort of curtain above it. Then I had a feeling, much like a spider's web sliding over my neck, then something like a chocolate or a piece of cheese was slid across my lips. Yes there definitely was another woman present in the room and she was behind me. Then a pungent smell wafted under my nose. I was inclined to think that Madam Stringlet wanted me to pass out, or at least become woozy.

An eerie silence followed for several minutes until a soft high pitched voice asked me to put out my hands. This I did. "Turn the palms upward" I was told. Then more sensations followed. Probably rabbit fur or some kind of feather tickled my palms, not an unpleasant sensation, rather nice and I was definitely feeling much more relaxed, I felt some bony fingers caressing my hands for some time. "These hands have done some really hard work for a long time, probably in the mining industry." Then more silence, which gave me time to think that Muriel had been talking to her on the way over and had related to her my life's story. "There are lots of people wanting to contact you Bill. Firstly your mother Rosie wants to thank you for helping her get settled in at Aunty Dolly's house in Albany. She knows you came to see her after your father passed away, but she couldn't mouth the words, she had lost her speech and was powerless to do anything about it. She cried after you left but soon after she was reunited with your father and she has told me that she is now happy. Aunty Dolly is with them. They talk a lot together and laugh a lot, which she didn't have much of when she was here, left alone for so long whilst you and your father went searching for those illusive black veins of cassiterite."

When I heard this I was gobsmacked. Muriel didn't know all this. I became much more interested. I waited for Mrs Stringlet to say something. I noticed that her voice had changed and was not so high pitched, in fact I think it sounded just like my mother was when she was younger, mellower with a German accent. I saw flashes of a past life, the little school, Miss Higgins, Dad, the aluminium ladder, the stretcher and the canvas sheet, the long drive to Kalgoorlie. I waited and waited. "Do you want to say anything to your mother" I was asked.

I found it difficult to say anything but managed to get out "Thank her for being my mum" My palms were sweaty, so I took out my handkerchief and dried them and my eyes as I had become very emotional. Never did I realise that it was possible to contact the departed. Peace and tranquillity descended over the darkness of that room that evening. I was transported to another planet. I spoke to Lucy, Lludmila, who unknown to me had made lots of money, had returned to Latvia, only to die from complications of a gallbladder operation. Then I spoke to Elaine Woodbridge who was continuing with her good work for the under privileged.

Finally, as Mrs Stringlet was stroking the back of my hands, she said "Bill, you have been a very gullible man most of your life. But you have made a few people happy along the way. Your time here on Earth is less than I have got, so make the most of it. Nice to have met you and thank you for sharing your loved ones with me. Goodbye and ask the next person to come in"

I stood up, truly impressed by her ability to transmogrify herself so easily, and turned slowly towards the door in the darkness. I felt the door handle, turned it and found Wally waiting patiently for me to emerge. "What's she like?" he asked "you'll find out" I whispered as I floated across the dining room, up the creaking stairs and so to bed and a deep, deep sleep.

The next person who Muriel arranged to come and talk to us was a Catholic Priest called Father Eoin Kelly. I am not at all sure just what parish he came from, he may have just been relieving somewhere, but anyway he rode his bicycle over and was late to start. We had expected him to arrive about the usual seven thirty, but he didn't appear until around nine o'clock. He was flustered, red faced with a shock of white hair encircling his head just above the level of the ears, leaving the pate bronzed and bare. I heard Muriel take him into a smaller room off the main dining room.

"You'll have to pull yourself together Father," she said firmly. "Have you got the usual?" I heard him reply, "Oh yes, but you can't have more than two before you start your talk," Muriel retorted. After a few minutes Father Kelly appeared in our little waiting room, balefully glaring at us. He was a tallish bespectacled man about sixty years of age, agitated and slightly breathless. Because of the red stain on his collar I assumed that Muriel had given him a couple of the local red.

He blurted out to us as he entered the room, "Good evening, sinners, kneel down and beg forgiveness before it's too late." No one moved. "Behold ye to the word of God and get down on your knees immediately, clasp your hands in front of you and repeat after me" No one moved, Father Kelly was visibly shocked. I think that he was used to his flock obeying him implicitly. A morgue like silence fell upon the small gathering, until Bev jumped to her feet and started shouting, "stop this absolute rot at once! You don't know anyone here in this room, so how can you call them sinners?" She moved closer towards the Priest, screwing up her eye lids as if to see more clearly, "I have seen you before, Father, yes in Warrnambool, Victoria, you were our school Priest at the Sacred Heart College. I remember. Gosh that was a long time ago, and of course you now look older and more weather beaten, but how could I ever forget your face? You came into the girl's dressing room after gym one day, saying you were looking for someone, and you went over towards the showers. You were a nasty piece of work. The school principle complained to the Bishop and you were dismissed. Well, well you ended up over here eh? And you have the temerity to call us sinners. You of all people would know the meaning of that word".

The Priest, clearly shocked, pushed out his right arm as if to ward Bev off. Charles stormed to his feet and landed a right cross to the side of the Priest's head. He went down, backwards desperately trying to keep his balance, but crashed into Muriel who was entering the room with a tray of scones. They both fell in a heap against the wall. Wally rushed over and helped them to their feet. There was pandemonium. Everyone was shouting. Bev was shaking her fists at the Priest, who was screaming that "everyone is a sinner, and will burn in the inferno of Hell. All mankind is depraved as a consequence of the Fall." Muriel was yelling at Bev, Charles was gesticulating at anyone close at hand. It was just fortuitous that Bev still had her memory from her youth, as it saved us all from instant damnation. I tiptoed out as secretly as I could not wishing to evoke recompense from the Almighty, all the while uneasy with the Priest's hubris.

The next person that Muriel arranged to visit us was a retired English teacher, also living in Bunbury. She had taught at a prestigious girl's school in Perth before retiring soon after her husband passed away from a stroke. She told Muriel the name of the book which we had to read before the lesson, and which bookshop in Bunbury stocked it. Muriel came home with at least six copies and duly handed them out to the occupiers of Pennington House.

Personally I didn't find the book at all interesting, so I struggled every day just trying to build up enough mental energy to start the first chapter. The week before her visit seemed to pass slower than the usual. After wading through the first two chapters, I cheated by reading the final chapter, just to see how it finished up.

Anyway Friday night arrived, we all came down to dinner early, had our coffee and just waited and waited until the roar of the flattop was heard zooming up the side alleyway. Muriel introduced us to Mrs Kathleen Shyrock. It was obvious that she hadn't given a lesson for some time as she was very nervous and dropped her notes, which Muriel picked up for her. She would have been about sixty five years old, greyish hair tied at the back in a bun, wrinkled facial skin, from long exposure to the harsh sunlight, slightly coquettish, I'd say. None of us took an instant liking nor disliking to her. But it was her soft voice that kept our attention. Someone, possibly Wally, whispered that she seemed a very merry widow.

I was singled out to read my critique. Mrs Shyrock asked me to stand in front of the class, she saw I had no notes and became very agitated. She asked me why I had no notes. I stuttered a bit then said that I had left them in my room. She calmed a little. Then she asked me to explain the plot of the book. I looked straight at the other four members of the class. I froze. Charles was picking his teeth with a metal pick, simultaneously swatting an annoying blowfly, Bev was frowning as usual, and trying desperately to understand the goings on, Wally had a blank expression, was pale and I thought he was going to pass out or vomit.

Time seemed to stand still. I changed my balance from one foot to the other. "The plot of this book,(pause) is hard to fathom" I stuttered. "And why is that?" Mrs Shyrock asked purposefully. I turned and faced my accuser. She was in her element. She dominated our small group, she was back in the classroom again after all those years of retirement, she was the teacher playing with us, just as Blackboy probably played with the mice in the shed. We were being softened up slowly for the kill.

"Alright Bill, sit down. Now listen in all you lot!" she shouted. "Just think of the mnemonic PLOT. The letter P stands for the plot of the book, or story. What is the story about? L stands for location. Where is the story taking place? O stands for organisation. How is the book constructed? And T stands for the theme. What is the writer trying to tell us, what is the main idea or topic of the book?

We were then treated to over two hours of tirade after tirade as the Merry Widow shouted, gesticulated, remonstrated, iterated and cajoled us, acting out the various parts of the book, but to absolutely no avail. By nine thirty we were all asleep, Charles was snoring loudly, his woollen cap now covering most of his face. Wally was hiccupping and burping from indigestion. Bev was whispering to the little people, troglodytes from the underworld which only she knew of and spoke to in her dreams. Muriel saved the night by providing a rousing hot cup of tea, then driving the old dragon home to Bunbury, no doubt feeling triumphant at having embarrassed us all, sardonically, by our collective lack of knowledge about books. I am still waiting for the epiphany.

The next morning Muriel burst into my room, "knock, knock" she said when she was half way in. "I've just had a phone call, seems you are going to have a visitor this morning so you'd better get up and get ready. I'll watch you shave, so that you don't get any more cuts, today of all days" "Who's coming?" I asked, but no, she would not tell me, "That's a surprise for you" The unknown and the uncertainty got me going, so my hands trembled. She guided me through the shave, there were no cuts, handed me a towel, and some after shave. This must be important. Maybe it's Doug, I thought as I dressed into my cream shirt, red tie, and jacket. I carefully held on to the banister as I slowly and watchfully went down to breakfast, which was cereal, followed by a hot cup of strong tea, no milk, toast and jam, usually apricot, and cream if you wanted it.

I was quite anxious about who was coming to see me later that morning, so I returned to my room, made sure that the drawer where I had secreted my gold watch, was locked, and I sat down to make these last entries on my computer. Today, sadly, I feel as if my life is coming to an end, as Charles had alluded to, and so therefore is my story. I know that my life has been so self- centred that I never really had the time to have a metanoia, as I am sure Carl Jung might have wanted me to have. I have never really done anything of importance, I have never played football, played an instrument, or even sung in the church choir. Oh well, I suppose that is how life, for some, plays out. Muriel's strident voice is echoing up from the entrance, calling me to go downstairs, so I had better sign off for the last time, and go and face the future. I feel sure that this will definitely be my final entry, so goodbye to you all, and many thanks for reading this account of my useless life and escapades, together with a complete lack of a proper metier.

> Alas! I have nor hope nor health
> Nor peace within nor calm around,
> Nor that content surpassing wealth,
> The sage in meditation found,
> P.B.Shelley *Stanzas Written in Dejection Near Naples*

> The Moving Finger writes; and having writ,
> Moves on: nor all your Piety nor Wit
> Shall lure it back to cancel half a Line,
> Nor all your Tears wash out a Word of it.
> Edward Fitzgerald: *The Rubaiyat of Omar Khayyam of Naishapur*

EPILOGUE

HI, THERE, I'M RICK, yes Rick Dunbar. Muriel has shown me where my Dad kept his computer, which I now have. I have read his story, but I feel that it needs an ending. This is my responsibility, since he has now gone, to finish the story off, so that if anyone really does read it, it will be complete and not leave them up in the air.

As I stood in the entrance of that magnificent three storey wooden mansion, Pennington House, which would have been at least eighty years old, on that fateful day, with Muriel, the house keeper, I saw my Father gingerly coming down the creaking spiral staircase, from his room on the second floor. A thin shaft of light from an open upstairs window shone on his thinning white hair. It was obvious that his sight wasn't too good, and that he was so careful not to stumble. He looked about late sixties, stooped slightly, but immaculately dressed, in a cream shirt, red tie and jacket. When he was near the last of the steps, I called out to him, "Dad" I shouted.

He immediately looked surprised, and replied "Whose there?" "It's me, Rick, I replied, "no, no it can't be, I haven't heard of him in years, so just who are you?" he came back. "Dad, it's your son Rick, I have been looking for you for ages" "Good God, is it true? Are you really Rick Dunbar, my son?" We embraced, until Muriel reappeared and told us to go into the sitting room and wait until she brought us some tea and scones.

We sat at a long table, the tea and scones arrived. Dad was overjoyed and kept repeating to Muriel that I was "his boy" "How old are you now?" he asked, and "what are you doing?" I told him that I am a third year medical student at Notre Dame University in Fremantle, and I have just had my twenty first birthday. He held my hands, "there so soft, just like a doctors hands should be" he said "Let's start at the beginning, tell me what happened when your mother Lucy handed you over to her sister Kate, I only remember you as being about three, when we played with your toys, on the floor, while your mother went shopping. Soon after this she became sick.

I recounted my life with Aunty Kate, to him, until I was fourteen years old and left to stay at a friend's house. Aunty Kate had a lot on her hands, was rather cold, to all of us, probably because of her husband, Henri, who left us, maybe because he couldn't stand the noise young children make when they are excited. I don't think they got divorced, but he was really quite useless. However my friend's family were exceptionally good to me, and paid all my school expenses. He is my closest and dearest friend, and he is in the same year with me at University. He is the reason I am as I am right now. I couldn't face the future without him.

It took a long time to cover the events of the last seventeen or so years, Dad often wiping tears from his eyes. "what a useless life I have had" he kept saying.

"That's not true" I said "you have been an inspiration to me all my life. I remember you in your miner's uniform, big boots, heavy yellow clothing, and a big heavy helmet, in fact you scared me when I was little, but I have never forgotten you. I always knew that we would meet up again one day." "How did you track me down?" he asked.

"Well that was difficult because you altered your name to Bill, that threw me until I got onto the electoral role. That placed you both in Kalgoorlie and in Victoria Park, then you sold that house and moved to Star Street, Carlisle. Yes, it was very difficult and at times frustrating, but I kept on searching because I felt deep down that I was going to succeed one day. Last week I was in Kalgoorlie, and found Doug Hetherington. He told me all about you, I saw your name on the Honour Board, do you know what happened to him?" I enquired "No," dad replied, so I told him.

"Doug was a teetotaller, he had been invited to a miner's function, maybe he had a few, and after driving out the front gate to the mine, he was seen to turn the wrong way, to the right instead of turning to the left and onto the main highway into Kalgoorlie. He drove into what is called the grave yard that is, open shafts that have not been secured and so he must have driven into one of these open cuts and has disappeared, no trace, no sounds, just gone for ever. Dad didn't speak for a long while. He tried to stand, but was insecure on his feet. I then made a phone call.

"There will be a Flying Doctor plane here tomorrow to take us to Jandakot. Then we will get a taxi to Murdoch Hospital. I think you have pressure on your brain. I know a top neurosurgeon and he will see us in the afternoon, after you have had a CT scan, ok?" dad never replied, maybe he nodded his consent.

The next morning, Muriel, standing at the front door and waving, saw us off. "Goodbye, Mr Dunbar; may all that is good in life take care of you. I do hope all goes well." she sobbed. I saw her wiping some tears away. She and Dad held hands. There seemed to be a deep bond of mutual respect, even admiration, between them. Dad never uttered a word, but at the front gate, he turned around slowly and looked back at Pennington House for a minute or two, quietly reflecting perhaps on the really pleasant times he had had there with Muriel Anne McIntosh and Charles Alexander Appleton.

It took two hours to get to Jandakot airport, then on to Murdoch Hospital, but Dad had his CT scan before lunch. He held my hand tightly as we walked languorously around the corridors of the Hospital, but said nothing; was this a presage for Death,? until we found the Neurosurgeon's rooms. A great calm had come over him. There was now nothing more to be done. The die was cast. "Les jeux sont faits"

Yes, the scan confirmed that there was a lesion, about the size of a golf ball pressing on Dad's brain. "The op is scheduled for three o'clock, I think it is a gumma. Tertiary stage of Syphilis" the surgeon mused. Before we left he checked dad for lesions in his heart, skin and testes. He was declared fit enough for the operation. I was allowed to attend.

Before Dad was wheeled into surgery, we held hands again for the few moments he was kept waiting in the corridor outside the operating theatre. He told me that he was so proud of what I had achieved, and wished me every happiness in my chosen career. He told me where his watch was locked away in the cupboard of his bedroom where the master key was, and that I was to take good care of it always, as it was all that he had to bequeath to me. It was to represent his heart ticking away in my hand. I felt that he knew deep down that he wasn't going to make it.

The surgeon opened Dad's skull, since he knew exactly where the lesion was from the CT scan. A necrotic lesion, much like the centre of a golf ball, welled up into the operation area, which the assistant sucked away, so that a thin capsule could be seen quite clearly. The whole procedure only took a quarter of an hour and Dad was conscious in about an hour and was talking normally, with a small gauze dressing on the top of his head.

Three days later, a nurse who was passing his room entered and saw him struggling to get out of bed. She tried to help him but he gave a short gasp, fell backwards and passed away, into an eternal sleep. "Sleep that knits up the ravelled sleave of care, the death of each day's life, " (Macbeth, Act 2 scene 1)

Her name was Elaine. The coroner ordered a post mortem, the result was, an embolus from a large deep clot in his left leg had lodged in his lungs, and he had passed away peacefully, just like Mum did, all those years ago.

Now it is for me, to carry on with the good work started by my father. I dearly would have liked for him to be around much longer, but one cannot alter destiny, we have our choices in life, sometimes we choose to follow the wrong path, and of course have to face any consequences.

Unfortunately this happened to my father, when he met Lidia at the "house on the hill," but the good he did for others will live on, and not be "interned with his bones." (Mark Anthony)

I feel empowered, now that I have at last found him, and have put him to eternal rest, in the Protestant part of the Ravenswood cemetery, close to his parents, that his spirit will guide me along a true and Godly path.

About three weeks later, I phoned Muriel, to ask if there was any more of Dad's clothing to pick up. I told her where the master key was. She replied that she would take the gold watch, the cream shirt, red tie and jacket and put them into a wicker basket and place them on the front seat of the flattop, and pass them over to me when she picked me up from the bus stop after I arrived on the Saturday. She also told me that soon after we had left on our way to Jandakot, Wally had had a breakdown. He couldn't stand the abuse any more. He went berserk, found a length of piping, and bludgeoned Bev to death, as she lay in her bed. He then sawed through both barrels of Charles's shotgun, making it easier to put into his mouth, and so he too departed, suddenly with a loud bang, from this life.

Charles may have had a stroke whilst shaving, as she found him on the floor of the bathroom. She thinks that he may have hit his head on the side of the bath, as she couldn't revive him. Pennington House remained very quiet until George Jones, the former German taxi driver suddenly appeared and asked if he could stay. George certainly had a reputation, because of his prurient behaviour but it was overlooked, since there was nobody left staying there. Muriel said that she has to cut up all his meals, since he has no teeth. Because I am busy right now, I haven't picked up Dad's clothes. But I will, one day, as Pennington House remains close to my heart. I hope it stays, not just three floors of dry wood and glass, but as a true "casa di riposo" where one can expiate uninterrupted, for the past, in an atmosphere of quiet meditation sitting in a wicker chair on the back veranda; watching the setting sun disappear behind the line of gum trees, leaving an apricot coloured sky; a place where one can reconnect with one's Maker.

Alas! It was not meant to be. Muriel contacted me to say she was now living with her half- brother in Albany. Pennington House had been having trouble with the power supply for some time, and the cause was still being investigated. The other night Muriel gave George Jones two candles, just in case he had to get up in the night and found the power off, so he could find his way in the darkness. She suspects that he did get up in the night, lit one or both of the candles, and then either stumbled or knocked the candle over and so caused a fire that quickly took hold of the old wooden building.

Muriel was suddenly woken up by the crackling of the dried wood on the stairs after it caught on fire. She grabbed an overcoat, saw that the path down the stairs was blocked, broke an upstairs window and fled down the outside metal fire escape, that the local council insisted they install a few years ago. In the pocket of the overcoat was her small book of addresses and phone numbers.

Three firemen who were on duty that night arrived about twelve minutes later. They had seen the blaze from their lookout. The blaze was so intense they could do nothing about it, so they just let it burn itself out, which it did by eleven o'clock in the morning. There has been no sighting of George Jones, so it is presumed that he perished in the inferno, just as Father Kelly had predicted. Yes, unknowingly we were all probably disciples of the monk Pelagius, and so, like him, we denied to ourselves, the doctrine of original sin.

Muriel is still in shock, she has no clothes, no money, no friends, no family photos, no heirlooms, no job, and only memories of a life time devoted to Pennington House, now just a pile of smouldering ashes. But she does have the flattop and her much loved three legged cat, Blackboy, who she picked up when he appeared after the firemen had left around lunchtime. He was crying, more about his late lunch, than the loss of his favourite abode. However he is a great comfort to Muriel, as her half-brother Frank is half blind, half deaf and uses a wheelchair half of the time. Was Blackboy the cause of George Jones tripping over? No one will ever know. "Ashes to ashes, dust to dust". I feel that this is just a metaphor for life. That is all that remained of Pennington House, not even the metal fire escape was spared. It melted in the extreme heat.

"And how are you coping, Muriel" I asked "Well I'm not that flash" She replied, her voice slightly shaky, " I saw the doctor the other day, because I have enlarged glands in my neck, muscle aches and I felt that I was in for a big dose of flu. The doctor told me that it was due to an infection by a single cell protozoan parasite called Toxoplasmosis which is present in most warm blooded animals; this has now been confirmed by blood tests. He has started me on antibiotics, but he has warned me that I may only have a month to live. It seems that the cause is Blackboy, the cat, who has already been taken off to the vet and has been euthanized. Apparently he has contaminated the soil around here, so much so that the locals call me The Cat Lady from East Albany. The vet also told me that people in Albany have been tipping their kitty litter down the toilet, and the Fishery Department has discovered oocysts of Toxoplasmosis in dead whales washed up on the beaches." "I am so sorry" I gulped as Muriel continued.

I listened to her explaining more things to me on the phone, as I gazed out of the window of my room. It was a cool clear moonlight night. I clearly saw the stars, one in particular attracted my attention, because of its brightness. I wondered and I wondered long after Muriel had hung up, about what Charles had told my father on the veranda on a previous cool clear night.

Isaac Watts(1674-1748) wrote in Hymn 47 "O God Our Help In Ages Past" Verse 5
"Time, like an ever rolling stream
Bears all who breaths away;
They fly forgotten, as a dream
Dies at the opening days"
Seems as pertinent now as it was then.

On the following Saturday, I met Muriel's half-brother, Frank Kneebone at her funeral in Albany, under a clear empyreal sky. Mrs Shyrock wearing a bright red cloche, and her famous French female friend, flaunting a floral foulard, *de rigueur,* were there. Father Kelly took the very short grave side service, wearing his heavy black cassock in the heat, about fifteen minutes in all, before he scurried away puffing and panting on his bicycle, his face having taken on the same colour as beetroot. There was a largish wreath of red roses from Madame Stringlet's garden with foam white and purple bell shaped flowers, comfrey like, around the edges. Frank said I should take the "damn flattop", so I did together with Dad's things wrapped up neatly in the wicker basket. I have exams in less than a fortnight, so I am going to wear, the cream shirt, red tie, and jacket and of course the gold watch will be in my fob pocket each day, until the exams are finished, proudly, as I try my best.

"I love youse all" as my Dad, Bill would say. Goodbye and good health to all of you. Rick Dunbar. December 2013

TAMAM SHUD.